Typical Girls

Typical Girls
New Stories by Smart Women

Edited by Susan Corrigan

St. Martin's Griffin
New York

The acknowledgements on page 199 constitute an extension of the copyright page.

Library of Congress Cataloging-in-Publication Data

Typical girls: new stories by smart women / edited by Susan Corrigan.
    p. cm.
  ISBN 0-312-20679-8
  1. Short stories, American—women authors. 2. United States—
Social life and customs—20th century—Fiction. 3. Young women—
United States—Fiction. I. Corrigan, Susan, 1968– .
PS647.W6T9 1999
813'.01089287—dc21
                                                          99-12777
                                                          CIP

First published in Great Britain by Sceptre/Hodder and Stoughton, a division of Hodder Headline PLC

First St. Martin's Griffin Edition: May 1999

10 9 8 7 6 5 4 3 2 1

for Claudia, Elaine, Betsy and Kelly

Thanks to all contributors and those who helped to find them: Sarah Champion, Melanie Coupland, Avril Mair and all at *i-D* magazine, Esther Windsor, Nicholas Currie and Jan-Carlos Kucharek.

Special thanks to Simon Prosser, Anna-Maria Watters and all at Hodder & Stoughton.

Contents

Introduction

Choices, choices. Young women face more in the 90s than ever before. There are career choices, social choices, sexual choices and perhaps most crucially, cultural choices. For when we choose our culture, we're faced with the dilemma: do we use our powers of expression to throw down the gauntlet to our peers, or do we spend our lives running one that's set by someone else?

This was a question I often asked myself in the summer of 1997. Faced, like so many of my contemporaries, with hype about how many opportunities were available to switched-on women, experience was actually teaching me a different lesson. Everywhere: glass ceilings, roadblocks, dead ends. This, from a society which calls others just like me lucky, privileged and talented. This, from a society which claims we live in an age of post-feminism, where the battle of the sexes has largely been fought and won. We'll forget those little niggles like equal pay and worries – no matter how attractive and intelligent any of us might be – that we still had to conform to somebody else's agenda to ultimately salvage any sense of self-worth from our own lives or work.

Once I saw this construct for the bullshit it actually was, life got easier. Work got easier, too, and *Typical Girls* was born. In clubs, at gigs, at readings, in galleries, in the cinema and later, when we all went back to mine to talk about it, opportunities presented themselves and simply said, *get to work*. I realised there were a lot of women out there marrying so-called 'high' culture

1

to an accessible, pop sensibility, capable of drop-kicking their genius into the future. They didn't necessarily need my help to articulate their message but I could provide them with an outlet where they would have a chance to be acknowledged for so doing. The rest, of course, was up to them. The lesson: nobody custom-makes an opportunity for anyone else to walk into; life remains a series of random meetings and coincidences underpinned by day-to-day realities. Chance is indeed a fine thing.

But how to convey the *frisson* of those meetings, the spirals of thought and the spark of connection which followed? The white expanse of the blank page, the dull grey of the clean slate: they create their own crises. However, to the articulate, these expanses are tools – weapons, even. I think there's something incredibly satisfying about having a weapon, especially if you're a woman in 1997, the weapon in question is a quick mind and your battlefield, your arena, your headspace is compelling enough to form words, songs and pictures that chronicle right now while planting the seeds of inspiration for the future. What's moved *you*, for example? Do you know what it's like to emerge from an exhibition or a film or a disco, to finish a book or a record and come out the other side trembling with enthusiasm and plans for the future? Do you know how it feels to channel those feelings into a creation all your own? Have you tried?

Typical Girls acknowledges the root of inspiration and the disciplines which communicate it. The book owes debts of gratitude to feminism, a movement which seeks to remind women of their absolute equality to men; and to punk rock, the fuck-you, can-do attitude and the catalyst behind so many brilliant books, songs, films and powerful pieces of art. These links unite the contributors collected in this deceptively slim volume and underpin their role as chroniclers of a generation's readiness to take on the world on their own terms. Although in many cases their primary means of expression comes to us through another medium, all of these women can write to further convey the messages they intend to send out. Their stories are worth reading. I wouldn't have it any other way.

When women tell stories, even today, there are still those who would pillory us for our choice of words or topics. Let them: the closed and hermetic world of this type of critic precludes almost any contact with the thrill and spontaneity found on the street or in the playground of the mind. We are all of us hemmed in by patronizing descriptions of 'autobiography' when men who use their lives for source material are lionized as perceptive guides drawing on their valuable life experiences; this is a double-standard which drags down an entire culture by suggesting to over half the population that the chroniclings of their inner world are not worthy of equal analysis. Would Kafka – to name but one example – be so judged for laying bare his own marriage of imagination and innermost thoughts?

Often – and this is crucial – it's the female misogynists in our number who hold us back the most; the over-cautious, over-qualified commentators who claim to want young women to do well, yet keep reordering the terms under which they are allowed to succeed. How liberal is that? *Typical Girls* rejects the empty world of the closed debate, the sad spectacle of the self-appointed regulator who ruins any chance to move forward by bemoaning the exclusivity of a culture they've helped to reinforce. The wiggle and giggle of pop culture has run riot over the last decade, crucially offering up a plethora of girl-powered bands and a landslide of artists who succeed on their terms alone; the worlds of film and television aren't lagging far behind. It's astonishing that this is not more widely recorded or articulated, but less so when we admit that other voices might be speaking for us on the printed page. Although female consumers buy most of the books for sale these days, few publishers cope well with meeting their demands for relevant books by interesting, talented women, much less with providing an impetus to get out there and write the books of the future.

Can this be, in an era touched by thirty years of feminism and decades of other forms of inspiration? I've always called myself a feminist but I'm not willing to follow textbook definitions of feminism to put my point across. If anything, I'm a kamikaze feminist using every opportunity to work towards a world where equality renders the term obsolete; I am not threatened by the idea of my own redundancy in a post-feminist world because I know I'll always have something to say and the ability to move a dialogue forward. I would much rather be one of those catalysers who sees routes and possibilities and paths which open what I like to call 'the door upstairs' and I know smart girls who can help me realize this.

The world we're looking at every day is bigger than some marketing executive's concept of Girl Power underpinned by naughtiness and rebellion. Being female and equal isn't about transgression any more. Women have been bad, naughty, subversive and rebellious for decades; bad girls, rebel girls and their ilk have an uncertain place in a world where young women, convinced of their convictions and their rights, don't see self-assertion as a sneaky crime against a patriarchal society. If we did, this would be a back-handed admission that a cautious society attempting to confine the expression of every person was actually acting with deserved authority, doing the right thing. *Typical Girls* is but one manifestation of assertiveness and expression, an interconnected, yet independent link to a future

Introduction

where women take their rightful, pivotal role. Or it's a collection of vibrant, intelligent writing with more than its fair share of wit, verve and style. Either way, it works.

So all those days spent looking for peers whose attitudes and talents underscore this passionate stab at looking at the world from a girl's-eye view and all those nights spent out on the tiles forging the bonds that brought us all together, won't have been in vain. Women now enjoy more control and real power over their situations than they ever have; creatively, this opening of the floodgates leaves more 'doors upstairs' open than there ever were in the so-called age of chivalry. And *après le déluge?* Leave a light on, and make sure those doors are never slammed shut.

Susan Corrigan
London
Summer 1997

Bidisha

'TALKING IN BED'

The light above the sink doesn't work, winking at me from behind its plastic hood, its long white eye peeking, eking out a millisecond of brightness. Inside the uncleared bin lie three used tampons carelessly wrapped in cheap notepaper grizzled with old Biro slashes, through which seeping burgundy maps out scum-encrusted estuaries thick with smell. The greyness of the concrete platform beneath the window-chipped paint, jammed an inch open, is only relieved by the star-print of a browning plant which sits in its terracotta pot, brooding in a night whose half-closed moon looks sidelong at a wavering patchwork-sample of cloud.

The twilight stoops closer to snuff out the city; there are calls and laughs from below as someone throws something metallic which skitters and is then flattened under a masculine boot-print. A knock on the door and my automatic answer: 'Hi, come in.'

A boy walks in and hovers behind his cigarette's sparkler-trails in the dim, and I listen to his low voice coughing, which resonates past boy and adult, even, so each word clappers dull-vowelled on my ear drums. His thick tongue slaps out across his lips, doubles back pink-rippling across teeth grey and haphazard as a fortress-ruin, as he stutters a greeting rehearsed in the brown air of the corridor outside.

Smirnoff shines whitely into the tumblers I've set out, squat and promising as crystal Buddha figurines, and we toast the city, which rises up around us with its bland brownness of vision, its narrowly blind windows and choking stones, the soft echoes in

9

the endless alleys enmeshing the town, which is coldly dark and now reverberates with the nearby chapel's bells. More Smirnoff silvers around our glasses, this time neat, and skates down my throat mumbling its bitter-voiced lullaby; leopard-like it purrs and curls inside my stomach, flipping its tail-end high in my mouth, claws secretly scarring the pulpy inside . . . which moves of its own accord; more red ejects and soaks below.

Nobody warned me about this unmoving air, the thirty pubs frozen in time, the domino-march of boys in tuxedos every Saturday night, the weekly bops crusty with hired satin, with chalky ankles bulging from two-strap sandals. Boredom mists and fumes inside this room as I sit for entire bland afternoons gripping and gnashing at my desk. I hope one day that those brown-bricked spires erupt in mushroom-clouds of crinkling parchment and shattered stained glass, that the thousand bikes clatter to their rusted decline against the broad glassy back of a modern cab, a bus with its noxious breath. No more college scarves, no more great skin. No teenaged ploy, no tantrum, tears or slamming doors can get me away, for this is the escape I envisioned for the last two years.

Of course I've tried the escape option, the poets' route, the zenith of existentialist thought at age thirteen in the tackiest way possible: twenty, thirty pills sweetly Union Jack blue and sugarcube white, glossy with plastic innocence . . . which made me sleep sick and greenly cold for a day and night, pulled through ancient dreamscapes the most barren land, the most elemental structures by a battling and raw-knuckled subconscious . . . I woke up, the wide red rim of a bucket held by my mother's hands up to my face. But that private decline isn't me: I want to launch myself from a window-ledge at the height of noon in the scalpel-coolness of winter sun, in a scarlet velvet cloak, with my hair in curls, reciting Rossetti and scattering old love-letters as I plummet.

It's getting later: a shark pack of men's footfalls beat past my door; down the corridor someone gags and chokes and amber-green semi-liquid sprays the toilet; a girl's laugh sirens up the stairs and female shoes stapler-click, light and silly, tiredly giddy across the landing; a couple huddle in a corner, red tongues windscreen-wiping from side to side, cheeks billowing and tightening like bellows. In my room, he is sprawled, denim legs wide apart. In ten years' time . . . maybe twenty . . . vision slips and flickers sublimely. The woken preying feline of vodka in me prowls and stretches; now it feels the clean black shine of night. My feet are burning in their shoes, palms are scratch-pads of swelling skin, earlobes itch; more blood; each vertebra expands and jostles for space, a white marshmallow of mash-enfolded semi-solid, slipping and rocking.

Outside, the corridor smells of stale piss and vomit. The rubberized black floor feels spongy to my bare feet while the walls undulate sullenly, in limbo-folds and stripper-wriggles. I look down, over the brass banister, at the domino-fall of black steps and the bottom-edge of door which leads to the outside. My spit disappears like a shooting star down past the two other landings; I don't see it hit the ground. A boy is coming up the stairs foreshortened, unaware with a tide of opal bright hair and ruby lips, languidly slanting sable eyebrows and beguiling nostrils. I look at the snow-slopes of his skin and shake my head when he asks if I've seen . . . she lives on this corridor . . . do you know? I shrug, looking at the daring jumper which fits sleek as fox fur, those black shoes like pristine coffins each clasping a cold blue foot. His smile fills the landing with celestial flame and I almost curtsey.

I am in the puking cubby-hole, the spew-corner, the vomit-cell. I balk, and a white stream vaults out of my throat into the bowl, flecked with creamy brown: hot chocolate, microwaved pasta. Some molten crystals explode vividly next: herbal tea, fruit juice. I watch the colours separate and mix; in the next cubicle someone is shitting violently. The commode slowly stops spinning, the burning tiles cool, the lino flattens. Pellets of gummy regurgitant are tangled in my hair, swinging like hippy beads.

Back in my room I excuse myself and brush my teeth quickly underneath the impotent tube light, which blanks and brights yellow on and off until my vision is a Warhol exhibition of self-portrait negatives. The toothbrush makes me gag one more time and I retch feverishly into the basin slightly disappointed — nothing forthcoming except green ooze. If I can get through this . . .

He has finished the Smirnoff and talks to me in an unpunc-tuated stream, his loose cotton shirt the colour of oxblood, unfashionable, spread like a killing-field over a chest whose flatnesses I try to imagine, but can only think of the limp cleanness of tarpaulin, the flimsiness of vinyl, the damp flap of drying bed sheets.

Masculine strength, though it may be there in a tendon-maze of piston-force and iron-like compressed tension, is always hard to contemplate. Hair streaks across his forehead and over the ears, syrup fading to the creamy white of candle wax, as his untrained, unhardened voice prattles deeply on. He has the vacant plastic stare of stuffed toys, the flaky one-dimension of chalk and oxidized copper. No storm of doubt will ever batter against that mind, which is as flat and unambiguous as black-board.

He leans back and stretches, like a maggot, fat and white and flexing. I watch him and something inside me shrinks, wringing out more redness.

Flaps of clothing drop – a button comes off and falls with a plastic snap on the floor, a stubborn zip growls between hasty fingertips – and his dishcloth tongue sweeps into the vents of my ears, the dry slope of breasts and crepe underside of arms. All his weight arrows into the twisted behind of my knee, which silently purples under my jeans; recollections of other males card-shuffle on the green felt of memory . . . the ceiling's browning in one corner, creamy-damp in the other, an old socket or connection-point prongs nakedly to one side. His hand closes over a breast and squeezes, like a spoon pressing into crème brulée; the nails of the other hand crescent into my haunch . . . he seems to know . . . I wonder what instructive book he's read, what films he's watched in the darkened gloom of his poster-walled bedroom, what his friends have illustrated.

There is always the backing-off as you fumble over the packet, on which two people so similar they are probably siblings share a hazy sunset and smile . . . I'm afraid I'll have to ask you to leave. Sorry, this isn't a good idea. Why don't you – I mean – maybe next week? I'll drop you a note . . . His cock is the colour of raspberry sorbet, boiled sweets, lavender pot-pourri. He is on the verge of being a good lover; united, we're a forest fruits gateau, an overcooked blueberry tart, a pulped pomegranate stirred into oxtail soup; we move together like a kipper darting in and out of pink sea-sponge, like red washed garments being wrung into each other then flung apart. His teeth hole-punch from my ear to the pitted crevice between my shoulder-blades; his tongue wetly dots. There are noises, like the battering of moths against lightshades, the clicking of crickets, the bubbling of hot mud, rhythmically unspooling beneath his useless tradi-tional half-spoken words, the garbled compliments his larynx strains to form through the corrugated fog of screwing.

Two hours later I am lying on my bed, its thin sheets pulled back like skin peeling away from a wound, and watching him – whose body is not as dense-muscled as I thought it would be, but simply wide and flat and bony, like a starved cow's ankle – picking and sorting his clothes. His back is creamy, the solid white of cottage cheese and mayonnaise, and the sheets are a tie-dye Smithfield snapshot of gore; there are runnels and rivulets of blood, pools and dots, circles and lines of maroon streakage. I say something and he laughs but I hear the resentment; he wants to witness what he's spent his whole life reading about: the softness of woman, the watery gold of her gaze, the love pang and flutters of her satiny heart. He waits for me to ask him to stay, but Cupid isn't suspended in a dome of silver-shavings and gilded harp-chords outside the window, nor Venus seated on a platinum foot-rest in a swathe of burnished hair weaving a tapestry of our mutual destiny.

My mind is no abacus, full of bright blue clicking pellets and pills of knowledge and memory; it's a wide cracked basin whose bottom is scratched and scarred, with dull marbles rolling about randomly inside. It's a fetid swamp where articles hiss and evaporate in an acidic mushroom-cloud, or are finally dredged up slime-sealed and unrecognizable. Right now it's a square white canvas, a clean newly-opened diary, a patch of empty winter sky.

In the shower I clean myself inside and out. Behind the ears, between the fingers, the soles of the feet; the soap toboggans over my stomach, go-karts round my knees, pirouettes on the floor. More braying male voices pummel the walls: they must be

14

in the kitchen, slotting bare white slices of bread into their moist mouths, scooping out fingerfuls of salad cream, crunching cereal savagely. I turn the dial of the shower even further and the water war-marches full into my face.

The room stinks when I walk into it, wrapped in a towel. I squat on my desk, kneeing stapler and pencil-tin out of the way, and use my whole weight to pull the window up higher. I crouch, tidying away the day's papers, flipping magazines into order and binning the empty vodka bottle. I look at the postcards on the notice-board, the vases on the window-ledge, the books tight on the shelves; the night swills about in the room, not the endless sweet black of shadows and velvet curtains and freshly-tarred roads but something mesh-complex and spiteful which hulks and shudders, watching me endless and unblinking.

Before the mirror I reach out and caress reflected contours agelessly smooth; behind reflected shoulders wrinkled with pores and spots stares in the reflected black square of night-window. Blood puddles in my groin; I hear the boy, who has returned, breathing outside my door; I lean against the door and stare dumbly as he wrenches the handle from outside. The opposite face with its beauties and imperfections watches strange-planed . . . turns the lock silently.

His breathing hisses up from the gap beneath the door . . . turn concentrating to the looking-glass and brave the sneering, dry visor of an unrecognizable mirror-image . . . grey air hustles in, body-guarded with all the silt and soot of post-midnight. Inside the towel my flesh is a collage of sweat and flake, of creamy white shading to near-purple, abundant stab-me softness and the bold jut of bone; somewhere inside that shivers and whines a personality unembodied and unseen. Those spires carry on yearning up, pointing broken-slated away from the unchang-

ing streets and ancient turnings, the worn signs and meandering
river. In a hundred rooms smooth-fleshed bodies writhe and
buck, a thousand pages of Keats flip, more spilt sherry puddles,
the chapels' bells bleat, unhurried.

Jennifer Belle

'BOOK OF NICK'

Nick sat in his leather chair and thought about calling his ex-girlfriend. He thought about calling his attorneys. He felt like his head was going to explode. He had just finished reading her novel. It was better than he had thought it was going to be. He had to admit it was funny and well written but, she can't get away with that, Nick kept thinking to himself.

He read the acknowledgments which did not include his name, even though he'd bought her the computer she wrote it on. She said she never could have written it if he hadn't given her a computer. And a printer.

He thought about how he supported her for the first three years that she wrote that novel. He paid the rent. He took her to Paris where half of her book takes place. There was the scene where an African man compliments her jacket in the first-class section of the airplane. He paid for those tickets and that jacket. She wrote about all the restaurants he took her to, and the hotel, and their day in Versailles.

And she wrote about Nick, or 'Dick' as she called him in the book. She called him 'Dick' complete with the quotation marks. She wrote at great length about his penis using words like 'just okay', 'shabby', and 'middle-aged'. Nick reread that section thirty times in disbelief. What did she mean by shabby, he wondered. He had tried to be happy for her. He felt bludgeoned.

It was all there. His domineering mother. The time he lost his virginity in a car at the Indy 500 and got VD. The cold stare and cruel, far-away expression he got when he masturbated.

Nick cringed. He had read the book in less than three hours and hadn't got up once from the chair. He was angry from the first sentence. He was even angrier towards the end when he started to get an erection.

'Oh great, just what I need now – a boner,' he said out loud. He read on. It was all his material.

And he had told her he was happy to give her his material as long as he was suitably acknowledged. She thanked everybody under the sun, people he knew she hated, but no mention of 'yours truly' as Nick liked to call himself.

She wouldn't even give him a copy. He had to buy it in Shakespeare & Co like a schmuck. That afternoon he had stood in line at the cash register waiting, staring at her picture which didn't look a thing like her, and when he got to the cashier he found himself standing face to face with her friend Blake. Nick hadn't recognized him with his head shaved.

'I didn't see you at Guin's book party,' Blake said. Guin hadn't had a book party yet, but Blake hated Nick and wanted to make him as miserable as possible.

'I couldn't go because I was in LA,' Nick said. He knew that Blake knew he hadn't been invited and that he had to buy her book like a schmuck.

Nick couldn't believe they let Blake work looking like that, with his jeans ripped and not wearing a shirt. Nick noticed Blake's nipples and got a tight feeling in his stomach, wondering for a moment if Guin had written about the time he had let another boy jerk him off in military school.

'Am I in the book?' Nick asked Blake.

'Let me put it this way,' Blake said, 'I'm surprised she didn't call it *Book of Nick*.'

'Book of Nick'

Nick pretended to be interested in a small book of lawyer jokes at the counter.

'Oh, and Guin's working on the sequel,' Blake added. 'It's entitled *More Nick*.' He bent over and did his fake high-pitched girl-laugh and quickly counted Nick's change. He couldn't wait to call Guin and tell her how pathetic Nick looked and how fat.

As Nick left the store and walked past the Shakespeare & Co window with Guin's book prominently displayed, he caught a glimpse of Blake out of the corner of his eye, picking up the phone. He was sure Blake was calling Guin to tell her how pathetic he was, buying her book. It just showed that he had done the right thing to break up with her. She was too young for him and her friends were proof of that.

Nick opened the book to see Blake's name, one of many thanked profusely for their love and support. There was a time when he would sooner have cut off his right arm than have broken up with Guinevere, Nick thought. He didn't know what happened. She wanted to get married and he didn't. That's what he told everyone. He had this image of her pregnant that he couldn't get out of his head. She was only 5'1" and he pictured her with a huge, pregnant stomach and it made him physically sick to think about it. He knew if she ever had a baby she would get really fat and never get rid of the weight. He couldn't stand that. Throughout their relationship he had really wanted her to lose weight but she refused. While they were together, that is. Now she was thin. Why did I have to have her during the fat years, Nick thought.

He remembered how, after their first date, when he realized she liked him as much as he did her, how his heart felt like a living thing, like an animal. A dog rolling in grass.

Sitting in the chair, the one Guin had begged him to get rid of, he felt a stirring. Some movement. Not a dog, he thought, more like a clam. Small and timid, but alive. He hadn't called her in a long time. He missed her. He picked up the phone and dialled her number. He was surprised when she answered.

'Hi, it's me,' he said.

'Who is this?' Guin asked flirtatiously. She knew it was Nick. This was the first time she had talked to him as a published author. She liked to make a note of things she did for the first time, published. Did it feel different to brush your teeth published, or buy a new bra as a published author, or go to ballet class with a book contract? It did.

'It's Nick,' he said, with no particular inflection. 'How's the famous author these days?'

'Why are you calling me?' she said. Not in a mean way, Nick thought. He knew she could be mean if she wanted to be. Though not in a friendly way.

'I just wanted to say Hi,' Nick said. He was pleased at the lack of emotion in his voice. 'I haven't spoken to you in a while.'

'That's because we broke up,' she said. She could hear he was sad, he missed her. He had never sounded so emotional before.

'I just got the feeling that I should give you a call,' Nick said.

'You just got a feeling? A feeling just suddenly came over you?' Guin sat on her bed flipping through the *Village Voice* and smiling. She had been smiling to herself ever since the call from Blake. 'I really can't talk now, Nick, I'm expecting a call from LA.'

'Why, are they turning your book into a movie?' Nick asked sarcastically.

'Yes,' Guin said.

'Who's going to play me?'

'Well it's a minor part really, probably Danny DeVito.' Guin laughed. Her voice was more mature than he remembered. 'Did you read the book?' she asked.

'I'm still waiting for a copy,' Nick said.

'I hear they have it at Shakespeare & Co.'

All of a sudden he wanted to have dinner with Guinevere. He wanted to see her. 'Why don't we get together tonight. Let me buy you dinner.' He waited for her to say something but she didn't. 'Anywhere you want,' he said. He knew it would take a lot for Guinevere to resist a dinner. 'Come on, Guin, I'm a good guy.'

'Are you still on Prozac?' she asked. She was remembering why she hated him: his white underpants, girlish cashmere turtlenecks, the moles on his back and the small patches of hair, the elephant-skin bags under his eyes, his clenched ass, and the Prozac. She had let him keep the apartment with the wall-to-wall sisal and the gold curtains she had found at the Twenty-Sixth Street flea market. He got the vacuum cleaner and the views and fireplace and ceiling fans. She had packed her clothes and brought them to her mother's house and spent a few months with an old boyfriend, a karate instructor who had a tiny studio facing a wall on Fourteenth Street.

'What happened to that blackbelt you were seeing?' Nick asked.

'He wanted to marry me but I said no,' Guin lied. 'I think he's engaged to someone else now.' That part was true. She had run into him on the street. 'I'm getting published,' she had told him, 'I'm getting married,' he had told her. 'How wonderful,' she had said, etc. That was the same day she had run into Nick with his new girlfriend, who wore a nurse's uniform and held the hand of her four-year-old adopted Romanian daughter.

Guinevere tried to relax. Her adrenalin was pumping. She

was getting angrier and angrier thinking of that jerk Nick sitting in his white underpants in his ugly leather chair in her apartment whose lease she was still on. He had paid her ten thousand dollars to move out, but she had spent that money immediately, buying shoes and taking the karate instructor out to expensive restaurants.

'I can't see you tonight because I have a date,' she laughed. 'We're going to Brett Easton Ellis's Christmas party.'

'What about tomorrow then?' Nick said. He thought for a second that he was actually going to cry. He had lived with her for five years and now she couldn't even see him for one night. He was still finding her long black hairs on the carpet.

'I don't want to see you,' Guin said. She felt sick. She could see that her face was red in the mirror. I have so much money in the bank now, she was thinking. So much money. If she had only known then that she would have a best-selling novel she would never have left that apartment. She would have forced him to move out.

She could hear Nick trying to hold back sobs. She hadn't heard him this upset since the managing director at Nick's investment bank had removed one of the two couches from Nick's office and sent around a memo 'Re: Couch and lamp hogs.'

'How's work?' she asked him.

'None of your business,' he said, like a child. He knew it was a mistake the minute he said it.

Guin was furious. None of her business! Nick's favourite mantra. Nothing was her business – his annual bonus, his evenings at the New York Athletic Club, his business venture in Singapore, his inane fights with his brothers, his pornography closet, his top drawer, his depression. 'Drop dead,' she said and hung up.

Guin's mother came into her bedroom and touched her forehead. No one hated Nick more than Guin's mother. It was she who had gently taught Guin that the pen was mightier than the sword. She was a writer herself and taught a course at the New School called 'A Woman Scorned: How to Write for Revenge.' It was one of the most popular classes in the catalogue. 'You're burning up,' Guin's mother told her. She had a fever from the call. Her first fever as a published author.

Nick sat in his chair sobbing the way he did when his mother shaved his dog when he was seven. He went into his bathroom and grabbed the bottle of Prozac and all the other bottles of prescription drugs, the ones for nightmares, the ones for headaches which he got from the ones for nightmares, the ones for insomnia, the ones for gas, and he considered swallowing them all with a bottle of Glenlivet. He thought of the nurse he had dated as a transition from Guin, how she had told him to take a pill only with water, and he filled a glass from the Great Bear cooler in his kitchen.

He started to swallow the Prozac one at a time when he suddenly realized that he had not taken Guin's name off his life insurance policy and she was still his beneficiary. He spat out a pill even though they were expensive, about a buck apiece. Then he remembered that she would never be able to collect life insurance on a suicide case and he began to take the pills again. He remembered how he had told Guin he would never leave that apartment. 'Not until they carry me out in a pine box,' he had shouted at her. He thought of the night they had signed the lease and celebrated, making love in the walk-in closet because they didn't have any curtains yet. He downed all the pills and the bottle of whisky. Then he realized something. 'She'll get the apartment!' he screamed. 'If I die, she'll get it.' He picked up the phone on the round black table next to his chair and dialled the nurse's number in Yonkers.

'Huh-low?' the nurse said dully.

Nick told her what had happened. 'I think I'm dying, what should I do?'

'Who is this?' the nurse said. Her voice was high and grating. She knew it was Nick.

'It's me, Nick. Please, please, help me, I'm dying.'

She wished he would. He had used her to get over Guin and then dumped her like a sack of potatoes. Guin had everything any girl could want, she thought, except height. 'I don't think Prozac can killya,' she said. 'But you might not be able to get an erection for a while.'

'I'm going to the emergency room,' Nick said.

They had met in the emergency room. Nick had an enormous bruise on his arm. 'It's changing colours, nurse,' he had said, 'and it hurts.'

'It's just a bruise,' she had told him.

He didn't believe her until it went away. She was going through a messy divorce and her mother was in town watching the baby, so she had thought, why not, I'll go out with him. On their first date they had run right into his ex-girlfriend, Guin.

Nick got off the phone and struggled to put his Paul Stuart shoes on. Guinevere had hated the faggy buckles. They were neatly lined up just inside the door. Ever since he had lived in Japan for three months he didn't allow shoes to be worn in the apartment. Perhaps I was difficult to live with, he thought sadly.

He thought about what it would be like to wake up in the hospital the next morning, all alone. Visiting hours would come and go and still he would be alone. Guinevere would not be there with ginger ale and chicken soup from Katz's. She would not bring him a *New York Observer* and try to entertain him by blowing latex gloves up like balloons and offering him a hand job under the covers.

Thinking about the hand job seemed to sap the strength right out of him and he staggered back to the leather chair, still wearing his shoes. And what if he didn't wake up in the hospital? What if he never woke up at all? In one of their many discussions about his 'bachelorhood' – Guin pronouncing the word as if it were a flesh-eating disease that kills you within hours – Guin brought up the probability of his dying alone in the hospital.

'How will you feel,' Guin insisted, 'in a few years, when you're on your deathbed, alone and childless, and no one even returns your call to hear your dying words?'

He had discussed this with a friend of his at work, a kid in his early thirties who slept with a different woman or two every night and delivered the details to Nick on E-mail each morning. 'How will you feel if you don't get married and you're all alone and dying in the hospital?' Nick typed into his computer.

'I'll simply say to the nurse, "Here is a hundred dollars, show me your pussy," ' his friend typed back.

I should write my own book, Nick thought to himself. There was the time Guin shrunk all his shirts like something out of *I Love Lucy*, and the way she did ballet in a black slip on the beach at his house in the Hamptons, the way she couldn't sleep without her secret security blanket, the way she started vomiting as soon as they left for every vacation. But she was beautiful and smart, Nick thought. Perhaps too smart.

Nick was getting groggy. He stumbled around trying to find *The Complete Guide to Homeopathy* on his bookshelves. He could try a home remedy while he was waiting for the ambulance. Had he called an ambulance? He couldn't remember. He picked up the phone and meant to dial 911 but dialled Guin's number instead.

Her answering machine picked up and Nick had to listen to Guin drone on about her reading itinerary. '. . . after London I'll be reading at the Pompidou in Paris next Tuesday, and then back in New York for readings at Rizzoli and the festival in Central Park, but leave a message and I'll call you back.' He'd bought her that answering machine.

'Guin, please pick up the phone. I love you. I just took a few bottles of pills, I need you. Of course if I die you'll be happy because you'll get the apartment.'

Guin sat on her bed and listened to Nick on the machine. She was already working on her second novel and this would provide the perfect ending. She could go to him now, for research, but she was wearing her new glasses and she didn't feel like putting in her contact lenses. Although she loved the way she looked in her glasses, and it would be fun to let Nick see her looking so serious and so . . . what was the word she was looking for? So . . . writerly. She made a mental note to write a short story about a writer buying glasses.

'I'm writing my own book,' Nick said on the machine, and hung up. Guin had often wondered what it would be like to be Nick, to live life stuffed into a shirt and tie, without an ounce of creativity, with passion only for a paycheque. No, she would not go, she decided.

Nick remembered seeing Norman Mailer being interviewed on television. He had talked about how he wrote on a yellow legal pad in longhand and then gave it to a secretary to type. Nick took a yellow legal pad and a pen from his briefcase and began. He wrote 'Book of Nick' on top of the page and crossed it out after staring at it for a few minutes. Then he wrote 'Book of

Nicholas' and crossed out 'Nicholas' and changed it back to
'Nick'. Then he wrote 'I love Guin' and closed his eyes.

Guin was glad she hadn't thrown her old set of keys ceremoni-
ously into the Hudson River as she had once considered doing.
She was ready to move back into her old apartment. The funeral
ordeal was over with, the police sticker was finally off the door,
the apartment had been fumigated – Nick's body had not been
found for a week – and the leather furniture had been removed.
    She sat down on a box marked 'early writing'. She had
newspaper print on her hands. She hadn't finished packing and
the movers were late. Her book party the night before had been
a big success, and she and Blake had been gabbing about it on the
phone all morning.

Poppy Z. Brite and Christa Faust

'SAVED'

'You see,' Billy told the hooker, 'I've always wanted . . .'

Words failed him. He reached into his flight bag and laid the Luger on the scarred formica tabletop. The pistol was inert as the brittle drift of dead insects in the corner of the room – but this was an insect of machined steel and chitinous blue-black sheen, ready to click to life at his touch. And its sting . . .

Its sting could rule the world.

'I want . . .' he managed to say again, but his voice was a wraith, a dying ghost.

The girl raised bruise-coloured eyes to meet his. Ever so slowly, she nodded. And ever so sadly, she smiled.

The Luger was a family heirloom, a keepsake from his grandfather's war, an artifact from Billy's own claustrophobic Georgia childhood. It was a semi-automatic pistol with a six-inch sighted barrel and a chequered grip of heavy rubber, nearly three pounds of sleek steel filled with little silver-jacketed bullets like seeds in a deadly fruit. Granddad took it down once a week to clean and oil, not minding Billy's solemn five-year-old face hovering beside the armchair, Billy's wide eyes following every move of Granddad's gnarled fingers as they performed the intricate ritual dance of ramrod and soft cloth, thick unguent that smelled of metal and mysterious manhood.

'You see this?' Granddad had asked him once, cradling the pistol in both giant, blue-veined hands. Even at five, Billy knew it was a dumb question: the gun was right in front of his face, wasn't it? If it had been Momma asking, he would have told her so, and watched her mouth prim up with the dislike she always tried to hide. He had his father's logical mind, she said, and hippiegirl Momma didn't believe in logic. Or guns, for that matter. But Billy loved his grandfather, so he just nodded.

'You don't touch this,' Granddad told him. 'Leastways not till you're grown. Then it's *yours*.'

Six months later Granddad was dead of an embolism, a fat gobstopper of useless tissue invading his steadfast soldier's heart. Billy understood none of this at the time, did not even properly understand that his grandfather had died. No one had told him.

'Do you want to see Granddad?' Momma asked him when he came running into the house one day, knees scraped raw from the big girls pushing him into the grit and gravel of the vacant lot next door. He wiped the dirty tears off his face – Momma would never notice them anyway – and nodded. Of course he wanted to see Granddad. He always wanted to see Granddad.

Momma lifted him up and up, through the warm viscid air of Grammaw's parlour, past the shelves of fragile knickknacks and figurines Grammaw always told him not to touch, even though Billy didn't *want* to touch them; they were useless, not like Granddad's gun. The gun could blow them into a million razor-edged smithereens. Momma lifted Billy until it seemed his head was nearly brushing the cobwebbed crystal teardrops of the antique chandelier.

And there was Granddad, looking more enormous than ever because he was so still, his best-suited body long and narrow and somehow *flat* in the confines of the wooden box that cradled him. Billy felt his heart rocketing in his chest, a strange and fearful excitement building there, trickling down through his ribs and into his groin. *Dead*, this was what the grownups meant by that short, inflectionless, utterly final word.

Then he remembered that it was his grandfather who was dead, and it felt as if someone had punched him in the stomach harder than the big girls ever could. The air in his lungs went hot and searing.

Granddad's cheeks were so sunken that Billy could see the outlines of his false teeth in his mouth, big and horsey. Granddad's eyelids were stained pale blue, webbed with tiny threads of purple and scarlet. Granddad's nostrils were huge and black like holes in the earth; Billy could see tiny yellow hairs bristling at their edges, and deep inside the left one, a delicate scrim of snot. How could you be dead and still have a booger in your nose?

'He's just sleeping, honey,' Momma whispered, as if hearing his thoughts. Looking back now, that seemed the cruellest thing of all. She had made him think Granddad would wake up, would come back somehow, someday. But Granddad never did.

Within the year Momma was gone too. This was the Summer of Love, and she heard the siren song of San Francisco, of men who had never seen a Georgia dawn and never wanted to, who thought of her pussy as the gateway to the Goddess, not a combination sperm receptacle and baby dispenser. She wanted flowers in her hair, music and orange sunshine swirling in her brain, not the endless dull trap of motherhood.

She never found any of it. Hitching on I–95, she got in the wrong car somewhere outside Las Vegas, a haunted part of the desert just south of the Nevada Test Range. A skull turned up a year later in a dry lake bed, bearing the toothmarks of coyotes, bleached to a brittle sheen, flesh and hair long since stripped away. The remaining teeth matched her dental records, and they shipped it back to Georgia in a cardboard box. Grammaw had it buried in the church cemetery next to Granddad. Standing at the grave, Billy felt a dull vindication. He hoped she had known fear and pain. He hoped she had thought of him when she realized she was going to die.

Billy's father, he of the logical mind, was long gone. Billy remained with his faded belle of a grandmother, who always smelled of sickly-sweet dusting powder and lost time, who was kind to him but so vague that she could barely carry on a conversation with an intelligent six-year-old.

Each Sunday Billy was forced to sit through the slow torture of a Baptist sermon, enjoying only the lurid image of Jesus nailed to the cross, filthy iron spikes raping his hands and feet, acid-green thorns piercing the smooth flesh of his brow, raw infected gash weeping in his side. *He died for your sins*, thundered the preacher. *He suffered for you*. And Jesus' pain was all the sweeter once Billy knew he was responsible for it.

He heard the Luger whispering to him as he wandered through the long afternoons, through the resentful house, always avoiding the parlour where Granddad had fallen into his last long sleep, where Grammaw now sat drowsing away the hours until her own. The gun told him stories of his own strength, strength he didn't know he had, strength that would be so very easy to discover if only he would climb to the top of the closet, open the shining walnut case, wrap his hand around that heavy chequered grip . . .

It took him nearly three years. He had always tried to be a good boy, to push down the anger he had felt rising in him for as long as he could remember, churning like some toxic black wave. But at last the wave crashed and foamed on the shore of his heart, and he saw that it was not black after all, not entirely.

It swirled with a thousand oily tendrils of colour, iridescent and lovely, and if those tendrils were poisonous . . . well, then, he would learn to live on poison.

The day Billy finally made himself lift the gun from its nest of soft red cloth and cradle its amazing heft in both hands was the day he had his first orgasm. He couldn't remember if he had actually produced a squirt of jism; it seemed he'd been too young. But he never forgot the pleasure pounding though him like a summer storm, implacable and cleansing. It was so powerful he thought he would drop the Luger, wondered whether it was loaded, whether it would go off and shoot him, then realized he didn't care.

But he didn't drop the gun. He knew it belonged to him now, just like Granddad had told him.

Learning to shoot was more difficult than he had expected. He'd tried it alone at first, as he did everything, skulking into the woods to aim shots at tree trunks that seemed to sway mockingly when he sighted on them. The trigger wouldn't budge at first, and Billy wondered whether it could be rusted; then all at once it *clicked* back with a dangerous ease, and the muzzle flashed and the sound of the shot filled the world.

All his shots went wide, and the Luger's recoil left his hand sore. He masturbated with that hand, remembering the little blurt of fire and the smell of cordite, the huge hollow noise, the power pounding back up his arm and shoulder, sending electric tendrils into his heart.

But firing wild shots in nighttime woods and vacant lots soon grew dissatisfying. Billy wanted to use the gun right, to aim it and hit what he meant to hit, without crippling his arm for the next day and a half. As soon as he was old enough to go without a parent, he signed up for lessons at a firing range. There he learned how to brace his arm, how to squeeze the trigger slow and gentle. He learned to hit a man-shaped target in the head, the heart, the guts. The instructors praised the cherry condition of the Luger. One offered him two hundred dollars for it, then laughed at the stricken look on Billy's face. When anyone asked why he was learning to shoot, he replied *For pleasure*.

He began to let himself think about the things he really wanted to do.

The ad in *B&D Connection* promised a 'true submissive', an adventurer with no limits. Billy called the number, got an answering machine with no message but silence and a beep, and left his own message nearly as cryptic. When she returned his call her voice was low and husky, utterly devoid of accent. They talked business. Later that same day he bought a train ticket to the city where she lived.

Not until he was actually on the train, *inside* the train like a bullet nestled snugly in the chamber of a long-barrelled gun, did he realize how scared he was. What if the hooker knew he was a virgin and laughed at him? What if she was ugly? What if he simply couldn't bring himself to do what he had come for, what he had dreamed of?

As soon as he met the girl in her cheap hotel room, his first two fears were put to rest. She was far too passive to laugh at anyone. And she was beautiful in the manner of a well-carved mask or a porcelain doll, her skin matte-smooth, her features faintly Asian, almond eyes ringed with black liner, lips smudged deep red. Beneath the black spandex skirt her ass was as round and sweet as a pair of ripe mangoes. Her face bore no visible scars, no indelible pain, no emotion at all. She held her tall, slender, almost angular body rather stiffly, as if half-sensing some pain ready to flare at any moment from deep inside. But her spine was straight, her shoulders unbowed. The submissiveness was all in her bruise-coloured eyes, her mouth lush as an open wound.

And he had not even had to say what he wanted, not in so many words. The girl was already nodding, urging him on. She regarded the gun with an odd serenity.

'It's not loaded,' he lied. Exploding shells were illegal but ridiculously easy to obtain. The first time he got some, he'd balanced a watermelon on a pile of bricks and blown it apart in a satisfying spray of red and black and green. After that he got a hard-on just holding one of those shells in his hand, warming it in his palm, imagining how it could make flesh rupture and explode.

His eyes cut away from hers, dry and burning. Twin heartbeats pounded in his throat and the head of his penis.

'Fine,' she said.

His fingers felt chilled and clumsy as he groped for his wallet. Holding it beneath her line of sight, he opened it and extracted ten crisp twenty-dollar bills. It was nearly the last of the money from the sale of Grammaw's house in Georgia. After this he would have to get a job, or starve, or . . . well, after this, what did anything matter?

A small sepia photograph of his grandfather stared up at him, broad-shouldered and smiling in his Army uniform, three years younger than Billy was now. There was the Luger at his hip, sheathed in hard leather. Billy closed the wallet on the only person he had ever loved. He pressed the bills into the girl's narrow, bony hand.

'Okay,' he said, his voice hardly shaking at all. 'Here's what I want you to do.'

Now he was standing just outside the door of the room, in the dingy fifth-floor hallway of a flophouse in a city whose name he had already forgotten. They were all the same to him, cities; the downtown business districts of smooth grey stone and blind silvered glass, the slums and suburbs forming like ulcers around a larger wound. That was what cities were, the wounds of the world. Billy supposed that made him and the girl in the room maggots, burrowing into the world's decayed flesh for sustenance.

He dipped into his flight bag, tugged a rough wool ski mask over his head. He wore a pair of grimy black jeans, but had taken his shirt off and stuffed it in the bag. The night air coming through the cracks and seams of the ramshackle building made his skin ripple with goosebumps, his nipples shiver erect.

There was a mirror in the corridor, its glass cracked and smeared with sticky fingerprints. Billy's reflection was only a dim black oval, unrecognizable and sinister. For the first time in his life he looked dangerous – now that his face was covered, his soft, weak, almost pretty face. Every time he looked in a mirror he hated his mother all over again, cursed her for the bowed Cupid's lips and stupid round blue eyes, for the wispy shock of hair that fell across his forehead like spun copper.

Billy pressed his ear against the door just below the metal numbers that hung nailed to its surface, slightly askew. He thought he could detect movement inside the room, faint and slow and silken.

He took the Luger from his bag and stood in the hallway cradling it for a few minutes, loving its weight and heft, cold metal sheathed in overheating flesh. If anyone had come out of their room during that moment, he would have bolted and lost his money. But no one came out. It was just after eight, dinnertime, and apparently this was a residence hotel: the sad smells of poverty cuisine seeped into the hall, frying meat and sliced bread, the sickly-cheese aroma of canned spaghetti.

He pressed the barrel to the slow steady throb in the crotch of his jeans, and his skinny body shook with a rush of heat nearly nauseating in its intensity. He was a criminal stalking the night, incapable of mercy, bristling with murderous intent. He was a soldier, grimy and desperate, under attack from an enemy more insidious than any his grandfather had known.

Billy twisted the knob. It slid through his sweaty fingers, unlocked. He pushed the door open.

The girl was sitting at the mirror, her reflection indistinct in cloudy glass, brushing the long midnight spill of her hair. The brush slipped from her fingers, thudded on the worn carpet. The bruise-coloured eyes went wide.

'Who are you?' Her trembling hand clutched at the front of the filmy white nightgown she'd changed into. Beneath that, a lace bra cupped smallish tender breasts, nipples stiff with terror or arcane desire. She was playing along beautifully. 'How did you get in here?'

Billy showed her the gun and watched her cringe. Her face went pale and the irises of her eyes showed a panicky rim of white. God, she was good.

'Shut up, whore.' He spat the words in the cruellest tone he could muster. Tears darkened those eyes like a summer storm rolling in. Billy almost expected them to stain her cheeks inky purple as they spilled over, but no, they were clear as rain. With the Luger's barrel he gestured at the gown. 'Take that off.'

'Please,' she whispered.

'*Shut up!*' Billy lunged at her, grabbed double handfuls of fabric and tried to rip the gown off her. The flimsy weave resisted him. Enraged, he rent it with his teeth, filled his mouth with the bland dry flavour of nylon. The gown fell away. Billy's lips brushed lace, skin. His nostrils caught the lemony tang of sweat. Maybe she really was afraid of him.

If she wasn't, she would be.

He pressed the barrel hard against the girl's breastbone, just above the visible flutter of her heart. When she flinched away, he saw a thin red circle already pressed into the flesh. The ghost of a bullet wound. He thought his penis would soon burst the confines of hot denim.

'Take off your bra.'

'Please,' she said again, barely audible.

He jammed the gun into her face, into her soft mouth. The barrel smeared her lips across her teeth, and blood blossomed, spilled, ran in thin bright streaks down her chest. Her eyes were huge, gone from bruise to an impossible purple-black, the colour of rotting flesh.

'I said shut up!'

Her hands spidered to the frontal clasp of her bra. When he nudged her again with the gun's barrel, she undid the clasp and let the scrap of lace and elastic slide off her shoulders.

The girl had no breasts.

With the gun still pointed at her heart, Billy bent to retrieve the bra, stared into the gossamer cups. Flesh-coloured padding, with hard little dots of pink rubber like pencil erasers where the nipples should be. *Mastectomy?* But there were her real nipples, small and chocolate-brown on the flat, unscarred chest. They didn't sew the nipples back on after a mastectomy. Did they?

'Saved'

He yanked down her panties, heard lace rip and elastic give way. *There*: glossy black delta of hair at the juncture of matte-pale thighs, unadorned, unencumbered. Between those thighs he would find no threat, only fleshy frills and folds opening on an absence of flesh, on a hole, on nothingness. Right? *Right*?

He pushed her back on the lumpy mattress and forced her legs apart. He stared and stared; he could not stop staring.

The soft flesh was dimpled where testicles had been pushed up into the groin. A rubbery penis stretched taut as chewed gum, wedged all the way back into the crack of the ass. No, not *wedged*. Billy saw the gleam of metal and bent to look closer.

The head of the penis was pierced with a silver ring that entered through the urethra and exited through the little wrinkle of skin at the base of the glans. This was linked with a large safety pin sunk deep into a thick fold of the perineum. The piercings had a dry, elastic look: they'd been there for a while, though the boy looked no older than nineteen or twenty.

His eyes were still purple with fear, though, submissive as before. As he tugged the lush synthetic spill of hair off his head, Billy saw his graceful hand trembling. His real hair was cropped close to the skull, bleached an incongruous white-blond; the contrast made his skin seem a shade darker. His left ear was pierced with a number of progressively smaller silver hoops spiralling up the rim of cartilage and into the whorls of the ear, his right spiked with a single ruby through the lobe, vivid as a drop of gore.

'Are you mad?' asked the boy. There was no trace of mockery in his voice, only the same soft monotone as before.

Billy was utterly bewildered now. The ski mask had grown hot, prickly, the coarse wool damp at his lips and nostrils. He pulled it over his head, felt static electricity frizz through his hair, rubbed his chin and scowled. The criminal in him was stealing away, absconding with the jewels of pain and forced terror. The boy's slender legs were still drawn up and splayed, and Billy couldn't help noticing that his ass was still as round and sweet as a pair of ripe mangoes.

'Punish me then,' said the boy.

Billy blew out a long pent-up breath. The room, the building, the entire world seemed to have suddenly gone inverse. The gun dangled all but forgotten at his side, his hand still curled loosely around the grip but no good strength to it, no raw singing power.

'What's your name?' he said at last, stupidly, almost shyly. He realized he had not thought to ask before.

'Jesus.'

Hispanic, then, maybe; not Asian. But the boy pronounced the name as they had done at the Baptist church Billy's grandmother had dragged him to, in the sermons he'd hated except when the preacher detailed the agony of the wounded man on the cross, as it had been intoned over Granddad's coffin in the parlour that day. Not Hay-SEUSS but JEE-zus.

Billy pictured a sacred heart pierced with thorns, limned in scarlet flame, dripping lurid blood. No Baptist icon this, but Roman Catholic by way of a Georgia tattoo parlour. He imagined jamming the Luger's barrel up against it and blowing it into a million chunks of useless twitching muscle. He thought again of that figure on the cross, pale and thin and pierced: a true submissive, a submissive for all humanity. He remembered a line of graffiti he'd seen scrawled in the men's room at Port Authority once: *Sure Jesus loves you, but will he swallow?*

He realized he had not lost his hard-on.

'Okay,' he said, a little cautious but still eager. It wasn't as if

44

he'd ever been with anyone at all; he didn't *know* what he liked. Maybe it could still be good. Boy, girl, what did it matter? Inside the fragile envelope of skin they were much the same. Jesus' body was a mirror image of Billy's own; bleach the raven tuft of his pubic hair, yank the genital hardware, and from the neck down they would be twins.

He slid the gun's barrel under the flaccid shaft and pulled up. Jesus moaned, shifted his bony hips on the mattress. Billy wanted it to hurt, and it looked as if it did, but the ring popped open just before flesh tore. Jesus' penis sprang free, already beginning to harden.

Take, eat: this is my body.

Billy realized the torn lace panties were still dangling from his left hand. He crumpled them into a silky ball and dabbed at the blood on Jesus' mouth. The fabric began to stain deep red. Jesus' lips felt slick and tender against his fingers, and those Oriental eyes glittered with – what? Desire, fear, pain? or some exotic blend of all three, some new emotion brewed just for Billy?

He knelt at the foot of the bed, pressed his lips against the velvet concavity of the boy's stomach. 'Don't move,' he murmured. 'Be still. Be quiet. Be cold . . .'

His tongue flicked into the cup of the navel, around the curve of a hipbone. The gun moved lower, nudging Jesus' thighs apart, kissing the dark sweet cleft of his buttocks.

'. . . wait . . .'

Billy's head jerked up. His hand flashed out and smacked the boy's face hard enough to make his palm sting. *'Don't talk!'*

Helplessly, Jesus gestured at the nightstand by the bed. Billy saw a large jar of Vaseline half-hidden in drifts of tattered Kleenex.

'Oh . . .' He blinked, sheepish. 'Okay.' He grabbed the

Vaseline, popped the top off and stuck the Luger's barrel deep into the opaque snot-coloured whorls of petroleum jelly. It came up glistening with grease, its notched sight nearly hidden in a thick coat of the stuff, the tip of its bore clogged. None of this mattered.

He eased the barrel back between the cheeks of Jesus' ass and found the tender hole, hesitated only for an instant, and sank six inches of greased steel deep into the boy. Jesus' eyes went wide. He sucked in a harsh breath, then let out a long shaky one; his penis gave a little jump and wept a single crystal tear.

As Billy struggled to free his own hard-on from the tangle of jeans and underwear, then kick his legs free of confining fabric, he felt the rest of his life peeling away. There had never been anything but this, no stuffy parlour where his grandfather slept in a long wooden box, no pretty mother who disappeared forever into the Summer of Love, no brittle bleached skull shipped home in a cardboard box, no withered years or husked dreams. There was only the giddy throb of his cock in his hand, only this boy's willing pain that flowed over him and into him, burning like napalm.

Billy felt orgasm stalking him, moving fast and close, then drawing away again. It had eluded him this way on so many lonely nights when his own hand was not warm enough, was not slick enough, was too obviously his own unsundered flesh. But all at once Jesus was tugging him up on the bed, nearly making him lose his sweaty grip on the gun. All at once Jesus was wrapping skinny arms around Billy's hips, sliding a mouth hot as an open wound around Billy's cock.

It was the nicest thing anyone had ever done for him. It was a feeling he wanted to last a thousand years, to last forever. It eclipsed his feeling of moments ago. *This* was all there was. This was all there had ever been. He and Jesus, their wet flesh melting into one another, the linkage of their bodies by orifice and cold metal, the mingled smells of sweat and Vaseline. The mattress beneath them was insubstantial, a cradling hand of mist; the tawdry hotel room shimmered and began to dissolve at the corners of Billy's eyes. He was dimly aware of Jesus thrusting his hips against the Luger, letting the barrel slide in and out of his ass.

Nothing else had ever mattered. There was only this moment, this unique point in space and time. There was only this boy he had met perhaps half an hour ago, and given ten crisp twenty-dollar bills. There was only the sweet ass inches from his face, glistening with Vaseline, accepting his love. There was only the gun, an extension of his body, of his very being.

'Do you love me?' Billy whispered.

Jesus twisted his head to look at Billy. His lips still encircled the head of Billy's cock, pale pink petals half-concealing livid purple fruit. His eyes were very wide, very clear. 'Yes,' he mouthed, and swallowed Billy deep again.

Billy felt a burst of light fill his skull, travel down his spine, go blazing through his balls and down the shaft of his penis. Then it was spilling into Jesus' mouth, and there was the answer to the hateful scrawl in the Port Authority men's room: yes, yes, absolute and indelible yes.

And in the final moment of orgasm, all Billy's muscles cranked tight. The long muscles of his buttocks and groin and the virgin bud of his sphincter. The muscles of his face and throat and scalp. The muscles of his hands.

The muscle of his trigger finger, squeezing slow and gentle.

He didn't hear the shot so much as feel it, a muffled shock like a fist punching raw meat. He felt Jesus' body jerk against his, felt a rending pain in his crotch as the jaws surrounding him clamped reflexively shut. A spray of blood and tissue blinded him.

Billy managed to get his hands to his face, scraped gouts of gore out of his eyes. He reached down and worked a finger between Jesus' teeth, pried his lacerated penis out of Jesus' mouth. Then he sat up and looked at his work.

Jesus wasn't dead. His eyes were bright with brutal awareness in his shock-pale face. His narrow chest heaved for breath. His abdomen was an impossible carnage pulsing with the efforts of failing organs. It was like some enormous steaming bowl of stew, full of glistening meat, splintered bone, great handfuls of tubes torn loose from their moorings, and everywhere the rich coppery sauce of blood. The sewer smell of ruptured bowel rose in shimmering waves from his body. Billy saw a gleam of metal: the spent casing of the shell, nestled in a dark purple loop of intestine. He had wondered whether exploding ammo would blow a body wide open like a watermelon. Now he knew.

Those bright knowing eyes sought Billy's. Billy wanted to look away, but could not.

'. . . you said . . .'

Billy leaned closer. He could smell his own come on Jesus' breath, a sharp clean smell that always reminded him of the traces of detergent in freshly washed clothes.

'. . . said it wasn't . . .'

A black gout of blood shot through with pearly threads of jism welled from Jesus' mouth, spilled over his chest. A long slow shudder ran through him, and the hectic light went out of his eyes.

You said it wasn't loaded.

Billy hadn't meant to kill the boy. He hadn't meant to shoot him at *all*.

Anger rose in him, immediate and caustic. Now this was gone too, whatever he might have had with this boy, another possibility stolen from him. *It wasn't fair. It was* never *fair.* He pulled the Luger out of Jesus' asshole, raised it and shot him in the face. The fine smooth features unravelled like a ball of yarn, painting the wall behind the bed with a thick chiaroscuro of grey and crimson.

He hadn't meant to shoot him *at all.*

Billy put two shells in Jesus' chest, watched it crack open and fly apart.

He *hadn't.*

He fired into the ruined stew of guts, then fired again and again. A spent casing landed on his thigh and left a long weal of burned flesh, but he did not feel it, did not notice. The body on the bed was little more than a series of smears now, like a canvas painted by a bad artist in a hurry.

Someone pounded on the door.

Billy pushed himself off the bed and backed across the room, away from the gun and the swampy mattress, his hands outstretched in unconscious denial. It wasn't fair. Nothing had ever been fair for him. He hadn't meant to shoot the boy, he *hadn't*, he had only tightened his finger on the trigger a *little* . . .

'What the hell's going on in there?' An ugly voice sinister as a slowed-down record, not kind to the ear like Jesus' soft monotone. And more pounding.

Only the tiniest *bit* . . .

'This is security. Open the fucking door.'

Billy's right index finger curled convulsively against his palm, scraping up blood. He caught sight of himself in the flyspecked mirror, his face and bare chest splashed with blood, speckled with bone and tissue and the fragrant contents of Jesus' intestines. Then he was at the window, leaving smeary red fingerprints on the filthy glass, staring five flights down at cars passing oblivious, at a Greyhound bus pulling out of the station across the street. Useless. He would never get out of this room.

Billy picked up the Luger again and lay down beside Jesus, in Jesus. There was one shell left in the eight-shot clip. He bit down on the barrel, tasted gore and Vaseline and the faintly spicy musk of Jesus' asshole. He closed his eyes and imagined himself asleep in a long wooden box, spinning in a void without weight, without care.

The pain, when it came, was a white-hot supernova filling the vault of his skull, then bursting it wide open. But it felt so much cleaner than the pain he'd had all his life. And it only lasted for a second.

Two bodies came into the city morgue early Saturday morning: a Caucasian male in his twenties, underweight, head all but shot off; and a male perhaps eighteen, maybe Asian, subjected to gross trauma by firearm. Both were unidentified, the faces gone to pulp and bone meal. The antique Luger was pried out of the white boy's rigid hand, bagged, and spirited off to the police station. The cop who stole it a few months later would have no way of knowing where it had been; he would simply wipe the sticky patina of Vaseline off the barrel and reload it with ordinary hollow-point bullets.

The bodies were tagged and photographed and scraped into adjacent cold drawers. The attending policemen forgot the white boy as soon as his drawer slammed shut, but they stood gazing at the Asian for a moment, fixing his picture in their minds. The morgue workers had been awed at the corpse's condition, and even the cops had seldom seen a body so thoroughly ruined.

'Saved'

'Looks like this piece of shit pissed off the wrong guy,' observed one.

'*Loved* the earrings,' remarked the other, with the air of one sharing a choice witticism. He had picked a number of small silver hoops out of the wreckage of the head before the guy from the ME's office told him to stop. Not until he saw a fragment of ear cartilage with something similar dangling from it had he realized what they were.

'Maybe we can get disinfected back at the station.'

'Don't scratch your ass, whatever you do.'

The cops left the morgue, bantering, and drove back into the clear blue canyons of the dawning city.

Tracey Emin

'ALBERT BERT AND ANDY'

Albert Bert And Andy

They were Squaters and we were Squaters
we had This in common - The hotel which
over shadowed our cottage, had once been
our home - Then one day Suddenly we
had to move out - The place was being
boarded up as my mum, Frantically carried
her furniture across The yard from The hotel
to what we called The staff cottage -
We never owned The cottage we just lived
There - Free - We had to, There was no where
        Elsse to go

I watched Them as They climbed up
on The Kitchen roof and Through The window
    Three of Them one Fair and two dark -
The hotel had been empty For years - From
The Front it was boarded up, but From The
back The whole Thing had a hundred diffent
windows - I'd watch The window it became
my obssesion - Every glimps I had of Them
became a secret triumph - I felt They Knew
I was watching - The hotel had six Yards, Gardens
All of Them Full of Shods challets and garages -
They were joined together by holes smashed
    Through each garden wall.

I got up early - crept down The stairs
and out The back door - it was day light
And The sun began to shine - I was going
to see The squatens - They'd seen me - I'd
seen Them - They knew I'd been watching
Them - my days had been filled with The
Thoughts of Them - one fair two dark.
I went Through The hole in The wall, and stood
    There -

The two dark ones, both with long hair
one with a beard, climbed out of The window
And stood on The flat roof - Hiya They said
and smiled, Your our little watcher -

    I stood There in my pink and white striped
nighty - not knowing what to say

    Doe's your mum know your here.
NO, No one does I said your my secret -
    They reached down and by my wrist pulled
me up onto The roof -

    I Followed Them Through The window, The
room was square - Three Lots of sleeping
stuff lay on The floor - a washing line
and some pots and pans, and a small gas
burner - The door to The room was boarded up
    From inside -
whats your name, The one with The beard asked
    TRAcey, I'm TRAcey

56

Smiling he said well pleased to meet you
Trakey - Im Albert This here is Bernt
and This is Andy - They were From a
place called Manchester - They'ed come
down to Margate For The summer to
Find work - I liked The way They spoke
It was different - They were different -
I stood There in my pink and white striped
nighty - Knowing There was some danger in
being There - but also Knowing not to be
afraid.
They were my secret - like I had invented
Them - The dream of an eleven year old girl
The Three wize men - And Albert, he looked
like Jesus with his long dark hair Full
moustache and beard.
Every morning before school, Id creep
out of bed down The stairs out across The
yard and Through The hole in The wall
And climb up onto The roof, sometimes
taking Them slices of bread, tea bags buiscuts
Anything I could get from The kitchen without
being noticed -
We'd play The little radio, and sometimes
dance - me a little girl in my pink and
white striped nighty, dancing around a radio
with The Three wize kings.

They showed me card tricks, and I'd snuggle
up in their sleeping stuff - while they told
me about the places I'd never heard of and
their lives on the road.

The four of us bound in this early morning
secret ritual -

Sometimes when Albert would lift me onto
the roof - his arms around my ribs, I would
look into his eyes - they were soft and brown
with long lashes - Gentle like a puppy
like he'd never hurt me, I was in LOVE.

School had finished it was summer holidays.
Mum worked as a chambermaid - she'd
be gone by 6.30 in the morning -

You see this coin said Albert, you can
have it - if you can roll it all the way down
your face - like this - he ~~rolled~~ held the coin
in his hand, and while I watched he rolled it
from the top of his ~~fore~~ forehead, down the centre
of his nose across his lips over his beard
and down his neck -
I liked it the silver rolling across his skin
He passed the coin to Bert and Andy and
they did the same -
The four of us sat there cross legged -
on the floor -

Taking part in some ancient ceremony
  Close your eyes said Albert, And keep
Them closed - he passed The coin into
They palm of my hand - And slowly I rolled
  It down The centre of my face
  I opened my eyes, They were laughing
  and giggling - A big smile spread
  across my face -

Christ said Albert, A noise from hell,
A pick Ax swung its way Through The door
  SMASH, - BITS of wood flew through
The air - I was screaming, it seemed like
hundreds of foot steps and shouts could
  be heard every where -

    Albert swept me up in his arms, passed
me Through The window - And holding my
wrist dropped me from The roof -
    RUN - RUN run he was shouting - I
stumbled my way across The yard - Through
  The hole in The wall, and into The arms
  of a police man -
    I wriggled and and tried to slip Through
Those hands - my nighty was torn
      And blood ran down my shins -

59

I wouldn't tell the police anything – They kept
going on and on – but I wouldn't say
      A word – And as Albert, Bent and Andy
were taken away in cuffs – I beg
      began to cry –
And all the police kept asking me was
How did I get the line –
      In a smouttering of tears I said
what line – They passed me a mirror
      And there From the top of my brow
to the bottom of my chin was a perfect.
      Silver line.

Tracey Emin 1997.

60

Kristin Hersh

'THE SNOWBALLING OF ALT.ROCK'

I've been asked a few gazillion times what alternative music is . . . usually by a journalist who bitterly suspects that there really is no such thing and would like a partner in this theory. My definition is always something in between, 'music nobody likes' and 'music everybody pretends to like.' The problem is, of course, what's it an alternative TO? Is it still underground if it's above ground?

Though it's kind of sweet that the industry has a way of saying, 'I don't know WHAT it is they play – how do they dress?' And it's nice that we always have an impression of stuff going on under the surface.

But what I really need is an analogy . . . 'Alternative rock is like a BIG ANT' or 'Alternative rock is THE McDONALDS OF THE FUTURE.' See, I can think up a lot of analogies, I just can't seem to relate them to music in any way. Music MIGHT be like a big ant, but I have no idea why.

Anyway, like many people with no real job, I do most of my thinking at the beach, where I often have to step over big piles of horse shit. This horse shit always makes me think, 'There are real moms in this world. Moms who stand in front of the TV and say, "Kids, go get your riding gear, we're going to watch the sun set on horseback this evening!" ' I can continue this fantasy indefinitely, but you get the picture: I'm a fake mom. I LIKE TV and we NEVER go horseback riding.

Once, my husband Billy and I got to see one of these fantasy rides at the beach. There were eight or nine horses with riders, all looking utterly miserable, plodding around in a little confused circle. They were led by a giant woman with flowing red hair who definitely had a few fantasies of her own going on. She rode a handsome stallion and was on a kind of Lady Godiva meets Annie Oakley planet. In her mind, she wore nothing but a cowboy hat and spurs and she was FLYIN'. In reality, she was trying to get a bunch of tourists on horseback to stand in a straight line. One man was actually riding sideways, his legs wrapped around the belly of his horse, his glasses askew.

The unhappy riders were a cross-section of planet earth; all colours, shapes and sizes were represented. The only two things they had in common were their original desire to ride a horse on a beach and their present desire to go home.

Finally, humans and beasts arranged themselves in such a way as to please Big Red and they were off. Billy and I watched them go by, one by one, and they really didn't look too bad . . . kind of like a bunch of sick, chubby cowboys after a long day on the plains.

Last in line was a teeny, little girl on a small, snow-white horse. She was the kind of kid that has horse posters on her walls, reads horse stories before she goes to sleep and begs her mother to let her wear jodhpurs to school. She was even wearing a little equestrian cap. In HER mind, she and her horse would never be parted . . . she would ride him to school, everyone would envy her and she would grow up to be just like Big Red.

Then she was immediately thrown. The white horse reared up and shook her off like a little fly. The only part of her body still in contact with the horse was a stray riding boot stuck in the stirrup. The girl made a terrible sound when this happened. It made me want to go to her, but Billy stopped me. The only thing worse than wounded pride is wounded pride and being comforted by a fake mom.

'SOMEBODY CATCH SNOWBALL!!!!!' Big Red yelled. Chaos ensued. The horses ran and bucked and galloped and the tourists held on for their lives.

Big Red might still have been happy, but Snowball was happier. The horsey revolution had begun and he was its leader. He was heading straight for the boardwalk, for the open road, into the sunset and he was bringing his friends with him.

Billy and I stood as far away from the action as we could without actually being IN the ocean. I think the word 'stampede' was mentioned a few times. Then he pointed excitedly at a naked couple making out under a blanket. Snowball was heading straight for them.

They looked up just in time to see a flurry of horse hoofs and sand around them. Snowball reared up on his hind legs and came crashing down right next to their heads. It was an impressive sight. They were VERY impressed. Sex was now the LAST thing on their minds.

Billy began doing the voice of the guy, earlier in the evening, 'It's okay, honey . . . nobody'll see us under this blanket.'

The other horses had by now caught up and were milling around the unhappy couple. The tourists were still gripping the reins, white knuckled, but now they were all looking UP. No-one spoke. I guess the horse people were too scared and high up, and the doing-it people were too scared and low down.

But I had my analogy. 'Alternative music is like Snowball, the Runaway Horse of Chastity.' Always running ahead, just out of reach, gracefully stomping our heads in, when we'd rather be having sex on the beach. You can try to make it stand in line, carry cute, little girls and unbalanced men, but more often than not, it's unbridled – heading down the boardwalk, into the sunset, breaking new ground.

Laura J. Hird

'THE BOXROOM'

As the coach lurched towards the castle, Carol looked at her mother and Uncle Len with disgust. Uncle Len was not a real uncle. Carol's mother occasionally took lodgers in the spare room, except the spare room was not really a spare room. Carol, therefore, had to sleep in the boxroom. A glass door with a wardrobe against it stood between the boxroom and the spare room. If Carol was not bitter enough about having to sleep in this windowless cupboard, she was frequently disturbed by snoring from next door. Uncle Len had first stayed there with his wife for a week one summer, but she had since died. Uncle Len had pleaded a broken heart and now visited every few months, free of charge. He was adopted. An orphaned husband uncle. His snoring was so loud that the glass in the adjoining door rattled.

Sometimes, while Uncle Len and her mother were having one of their private talks in her parents' bedroom, Carol would tiptoe into the spare room and take money from Uncle Len's purse. Although she did this almost daily, she would always begin trembling uncontrollably as she undid the purse's metal clasp. Also, her ears used to pop, as if she had been blowing up too many balloons and she could not hear properly. After taking the money she would have to lie on her bed (in the boxroom) until her legs stopped feeling strange. Suitably recovered, she would pull the stitching out of her teddy bear, insert the coins and stitch him up again.

Carol had only been recently moved back to the boxroom.

When she was very young, she had suffered from asthma. When she was first moved from her parents' room into the boxroom at the age of five she would remain awake until she heard her father leaving for his work at the brewery at 4.30 each morning. Then she'd run through to spend the last four hours of nighttime in her mother's bed. This was, of course, unsatisfactory. She began acting-out asthma attacks as she was put to bed each night. Her parents fretted terribly over their sickly little creation. For a couple of nights Carol's father slept in the boxroom and let Carol sleep with her mother. Every time Carol was returned to the boxroom the asthma would return. Eventually her father gave up his bed for a week, then a month, then years. Carol was thus an only child.

One night Carol said goodnight to her parents and went through to her mother's bed. She could not sleep as she had a terrible itch. She scratched until she was red raw but the itch persisted. Eventually it was too painful to continue scratching. She began rubbing rather than scratching. The rubbing relieved the itch but when Carol stopped, the itch returned. She rubbed persistently for several minutes until something very strange happened. Carol, for no apparent reason, suddenly imagined a policeman doing the toilet in a pram. Her ears popped and she began trembling but this time it was not unpleasant. She had felt similar feelings before if she lay down and needed the toilet for as long as she could. Carol forgot about the itch.

The following evening, Carol's mother was tired and went to bed early. When her mother had switched the light out, Carol began the rubbing again. She rubbed for several minutes wondering if it would ever happen again. Within a few minutes it did. The following evening Carol was moved back to the boxroom.

'The Boxroom'

Why did adults assume that children enjoyed day trips? How could they possibly imagine that Carol would be remotely interested in spending the day walking around an old castle? She had enough of that sort of rubbish at school. She would much prefer to lie in the boxroom needing the toilet, or sit in the back garden watching her neighbour walk about his house, or go up to the wasteland at the top of her street and climb trees.

As the coach rounded the loch towards the castle, Carol noticed a middle-aged man four rows down. Immediately she could not take her eyes off him. He was very tall and slim with greying hair, wearing a brown, tweed suit and smoking a pipe. Very distinguished. He was talking to a very old, small woman who looked as if she might die at any minute. The two figures were separated from everyone else in a luminous cloud of smoke from the man's pipe. Carol assumed that the old woman must be his mother. If so then he must not be married. Why would a middle-aged man take his mother on a coach trip if he had a wife? He made Carol feel all mumsy and brimming with love. She was eleven years old but was tall for her age and could pass for fifteen.

On arrival at the castle, Uncle Len hobbled with delight when Carol suddenly seemed intrigued and asked if she could go and explore by herself. They pointed out the tea garden and arranged to meet her there later.

The next two hours were spent at an almost constant ten-yard distance from the man with the pipe. The old lady's slow progress meant that Carol had plenty of opportunities to stare at the man's reflection in the glass of numerous cases holding jewels and suits of armour. If he seemed to linger longer than normal at a particular article, Carol would study it afterwards. She tried to build up some sort of picture of what kind of man

71

he was. One such article was a painting of Faust descending into Hell. It was the only article that Carol could make any sense of. Carol's mother had taken her to see the opera of *Faust*. They often went to the opera together for some culture. In each production Carol would get a crush on one of the male leads to prevent her from getting too bored. Afterwards, she would lie on her bed, rethinking his recitatives and controlling her bladder. She had done this now with eight tenors and a baritone.

Carol had enjoyed *Faust* though, as the story was quite good. She thought the idea of selling her soul to the devil in return for the man of her choice was splendid. She would willingly sell her soul for the man with the pipe who was now disappearing into the King's bedroom. Where did the devil live, she wondered? Probably somewhere in London, she supposed. You probably had to be an adult before you could sell your soul anyway. This seemed a great pity since adults would ask for boring things like new washing-machines or pay-rises.

Carol was much relieved when the man and old lady began making their way down the stairs towards the tea garden. The castle was rather dark and clammy and she was beginning to feel uncomfortable. She watched through the hedge as the old lady was helped into a seat on the lawn by her son. He then went across to the coffee shop. Carol sat at a nearby table between the old lady and the hedge. She toyed with her hair then leaned back in her chair, attempting to look sophisticated. The man returned with a tray, moving across the grass in long, lovely strides. He smiled as he approached. Was it directed at Carol? She was sure it was. In case he should look over again she assumed a constant grin. It was a look she had practised often in the bathroom mirror. He poured two cups of tea from the pot then raised the cup to his lips, his pinkie erect. He really was very, very refined, thought Carol.

Although she had needed the toilet she decided to wait until her mother and Uncle Len reappeared. She could not risk losing such an excellent view of this elegant creature. Staring intently at him, still smiling, she pressed her thighs close together. She felt her bladder twitching in a most pleasant manner. She lamented that the man could not also experience such sensations, indeed nobody could except Carol.

By the time her mother appeared she was beginning to perspire. Uncle Len limped across to buy the afternoon tea. He suffered from Parkinson's disease and was also in need of a hip-replacement operation. Carol could not understand why people like him could not simply be put down, like old horses. Her mother gestured to her to help him with the tray.

'Hang on, there's a queue. I'll go over when he's paid for it!' Carol deeply resented this intrusion. She savoured her last few moments alone with the man until her mother nudged her roughly out of her reverie and pointed to Uncle Len, who was now tottering across with the tray. Carol felt extremely embarrassed that she should be seen with such a person.

Carol's mother again shouted the order that she help him. Her tone was so harsh that the man with the pipe and his mother looked around. Carol stood up, thoroughly humiliated, then a sudden wave of strangeness flushed over her. She squeezed her toilet muscles but it was no good. She simpered and began running in the direction of the toilets. Urine was pouring from the vast dark patch growing on her lime green trousers. As she bolted, she saw the man nudge his mother, laugh and point at her. As she ran, sobbing, she heard fathers saying to their small children, 'Look, look at that!' and the children sniggering.

When her mother knocked on the door of the public toilet several minutes later, Carol was standing, naked from the waist down, wringing her knickers and trousers in the sink, sobbing uncontrollably.

'I can't go home . . . I can't go home . . . they all saw me . . . I can't go back on the coach . . . they all saw me . . . I'll have to stay here . . . you go home . . . leave me here!'

Carol refused to leave the toilets until the coach was due to depart. Uncle Len asked the driver to wait a few extra minutes as his niece was ill. Eventually she boarded the coach with her mother's arm around her shoulders and a travelling rug around her waist. There was a deadly silence as she made her way to her seat. Uncle Len was now sitting directly opposite the man with the pipe. The man looked over, slightly concerned. His mother tugged at his jacket to find out what was wrong. The man looked inquiringly at Carol then at Uncle Len. Uncle Len leaned towards him, removed his cap, scratched his stomach and as the coach stammered into motion Carol heard him whisper:

'I think she's started her puberties.'

Christine Kieser

'COMPLETELY OVERLOADED'

Saturday is the day to see and be seen at the record shop and the hordes have descended upon the Platter Palace. Punks with their hair done up in dangerous cone spikes come perilously close to poking others' eyes out as they peruse the 45 rack, looking for hardcore favourites. Gangs of straight-edgers with big black Xs on their hands yell at each other across the store and hold up records for their buddies to see. Other shoppers – who could be their parents – dig through the blues section. Our newest employee, Darlene, sits on one of the shoddy stools behind the counter, rocking violently back and forth in time to the Godbullies record that is playing far louder than necessary.

'So what are you doing tonight?' she asks, as I hand a green and blue-haired boy in a home-made Minor Threat T-shirt his bag of 7" records.

'I'm not positive, but I'm probably going to the Entry to see Babes in Toyland. What are you up to?'

'I'm tripping with some chicks from my other job,' Darlene bragged.

'No fucking way. I haven't done that shit in ages.' My jealousy was conspicuous.

'Me neither,' she says. 'I can't wait. There's an extra hit if you want to come along.'

Without hesitation I reply, 'Hell, yeah.'

When our day of selling Pavement and Big Black records comes to an end, we pick up a case of beer at the liquor store. Then it's off to the drug party. Once we're there, Darlene introduces me to Jenny and Sara, a couple of scenesters *extraordinaire*, who work at the coffee shop with her.

Chatting and drinking too quickly, and then, a bit nervously, we take the stuff. We distract ourselves by looking at magazines, all pretending that we're not waiting for the bits of paper to take effect. When it finally hits, Darlene's co-workers are poring over *Spin* and discussing which of the rock boys they would fuck first. Darlene and I look at each other in horror and recoil to the other side of the room.

Once we are out of earshot, Darlene turns to me and whispers, 'Whatever happened to "Don't fuck fame, *be it*"? That's what I'd like to know.' We laugh our heads off, all the while trying to keep ourselves under control. As stillness becomes cacophonous and the shadows on the wall take on a life of their own, we conceive a band of our own; we're thick as thieves over our schemes when one of the star-fucker wannabes pulls us into their world by informing us that they're going outside to search for God.

God isn't on our agenda. Darlene empties our case of Rolling Rock into her bag and we head into the October night. The full moon shows luminous through the bare trees, as the fallen leaves race the wind down the street. Our boots click arrogantly on the icy sidewalk as we walk briskly towards Downtown, and marvel at how much better the world is in our state of mind. We watch the breath leave our bodies without feeling the chill of the icy wind.

When we arrive at a park we collapse under a tree and open a beer each. Out of nowhere, ducks and geese come up to us expecting a treat. Miraculously, Darlene finds some stale crackers at the bottom of her bag, which we feed to them.

When all the crackers have made their way down their greedy little throats, our winged friends demand more. When none is forthcoming they turn vicious. By now, we are falling down drunk on top of everything else; no match for our attackers. Amazingly, we make our escape.

Since we've been drinking so much and laughing so hard, by this point we both really need to piss. Out of desperation we go into the bohemian hipster bar that we'd never set foot in otherwise. Darlene beats me to their bathroom and takes what seems for-fucking-ever as I wait outside fighting off the sleaze bags that inhabit this pick-up joint. Finally she emerges and I go in myself, close the door, and find myself in a jungle. It's only painted on the walls but I end up lost amongst the monkeys and birds in the trees. Only Darlene's hammering on the door saves me.

Racing out of there, without even deciding where we are going, we are unconsciously on our way to the Seventh Street Entry to see Babes. Despite not having the slightest idea of the hour, our timing is impeccable and we walk into the bar as the band takes the stage.

The show is one huge violent gorgeous loud swirl. Whenever I look over at Darlene she has a look on her face that completely mirrors the ache in my gut. Afterwards, we find that conversation with anyone else proves impossible so we high-tail it out of there. We wander the streets for hours, trying to fill the hunger we're feeling as the night's euphoria wears off. By now the sun is showing signs of appearing. We stop for a grilled cheese sandwich and hash browns at a greasy-spoon along the way, then head home for some much-needed sleep. My house is closest, so we go there. As I make Darlene a bed on the couch I promise to play her the best record of all time for drifting off to sleep to, when you've spent the night tripping your head off.

I pull out 'Throw a Sickie' by the Tall Dwarfs and somehow manage to get my record player to work. I jump into my bed in the other room. We each curl up under our own covers, listening hard. When side one comes to an end, we meet at the stereo. She wordlessly flips the record over and I drop the needle on it. We race back to our beds, and side two begins. When the record ends and the silence comes, we both lie awake staring at the ceiling.

That was the beginning.

'Hi Claire, it's Darlene. It's six o'clock and I just came home from shopping. I went to go buy some clothes and I had a menstrual emergency and ran into an ex-lover all in the dressing room practically. It was really weird. Anyway, I have class tonight until nine o'clock and then depending on how much self-control I have, I'll probably come home and study although I could probably be persuaded otherwise. So maybe you should call me and we could go hang out at the hip, sort-of-stupid place up there on the corner by your house, have a beer or two and shoot the shit. Bye. Oh, I wrote another bassline last night.'

It didn't take any begging or pleading to get Darlene to go to the bar that night, since when I called her back, the first words out of her mouth were, 'So are you coming to the CC Club with me or not?'

So there we are, sitting side by side in a decrepit red vinyl booth by ourselves, a pitcher of lukewarm slop in front of us. We are deep in conversation when we are rudely interrupted by one of the local losers who calls the bar home. Uninvited, he sits down opposite us and says, 'I see you girls together all the time. Are you dating the same boy or something?'

Darlene and I look at each other in disbelief. No one says anything. I try hard not to laugh. And fail. Darlene and I look at each other and then at his ugly, looming face. At the exact same moment we blurt out, 'We like each other.' The fuckwit doesn't get it, forcing us to endure his company for a bit longer before giving up and heading over to another table where his charms will be more appreciated.

'Hey Claire, I realize that you're not there, but your trusty machine is and you know how I love to talk into it. I ran into a whole bunch of people today, including Eric, who said that Tami is having a freezer treat party this weekend. You know, freezer treats, those things you wrap in tinfoil and put in a pill bottle and store in the freezer. Vitamin LSD. So anyway, if we go to Tami's it means we don't have to have a party ourselves and it'll be cheaper, three bucks versus the price of a keg or a bunch of beer. Boy, I'm more in the mood for the freezer sort of thing anyway, so it sounds really fun to me. I'm up for it, I hope you are too. I'm sure you are. You're my hot date for the Cows tonight, right? Call me, sweet thing.'

I'm putting yet another case of beer in the fridge, while Darlene is on the phone into the dining room ordering the pizza. 'Yes, just cheese,' she tells them. 'We want mushrooms as well, but we are mushroom connoisseurs, so we're going to put our own on.' She hangs up as I walk into the room and turns to me. 'They think that we're nuts.'

'Well, if they sold magic mushroom pizza we wouldn't have to go through so much trouble,' I remind her.

81

Christine Kieser

We drink beer and play records as we take turns walking to the front window to wait for the pizza boy. When he finally arrives, we thrust ten bucks in his hand, grab the pizza and slam the door in his face. We're as excited as three-year-olds with a handful of candy as we hide the shrivelled little mushrooms – our tickets to oblivion – under the cheese. We eat quickly and rush to Darlene's car so we can get Downtown before we are incapable of doing anything at all. Vertigo blaring on the tape deck and beers in hand, we drive to the Entry, trying to remember that a red light means *stop*. We find a parking space and walk to the club.

We're not even in the door yet, when Nick, the ferocious, sweet-as-a-puppy bouncer picks us up, one in each arm, his muscles bulging. Carrying us as he would a pair of rag-dolls, he walks us into the club and announces to the door person, 'Hi, we're Claire and Darlene and we're on the guest list.' He sets us free. We kiss him on the cheek in thanks and rush in to watch the Cows.

The place is packed but no one's there except us. As usual, we make a spectacle of ourselves in the very front. We dance with our arms around each other and now and again spin each other around, knocking over the innocent bystanders who are trying to watch the show. Afterwards, we are gross, sweaty as hell and covered in beer, mud and fuck knows what else from rolling around on the floor. We are the most pathetic creatures in the universe. We look at our happy, dirty, make-up-smeared faces and grin like fools.

Darlene grabs me and holds my face in her hands. 'Now, tell me the truth,' she says. 'Do I look as bad as I think I do?'

Stunned by the question, I reply, 'Are you fucking kidding? Just look at you. Your hair looks like snakes. You are so beautiful that I can't even look at you.' I mean it.

82

'Completely Overloaded'

We are invited to a party somewhere along the way. Of course, we must go. We are a bit tired from dancing about and making idiots of ourselves, so we revive ourselves with the LSD we brought along just in case. The party is a good one, despite a huge moment of terror when a horrible pink-haired chick comes up to me and says, 'You've been eating little pieces of paper, haven't you?'

I try to pretend that she's not there as the place goes silent, and every eye bores into my body, drilling deeper and deeper. Blood and pus are pouring out of the holes in my body and gathering in a pool at my feet. Somehow I manage to stop staring at it and look at the cause of my anxiety. 'I don't know what the hell you're talking about,' I say as calmly and normally as possible. Apparently I pull it off: she doesn't mention it again. The silence surrounding us breaks bit by bit until the conversation is at the same flow as before.

'Do you think they know something we don't?' asks my Darlene. With our pupils huge enough to walk into, everyone else's pinned eyes are too obvious.

'We know everything. What could they possibly know that we don't?'

'Yeah, you're right. I just don't want to miss out, you know?'

I sigh in exasperation and tell her, 'There's nothing to miss out on, believe me. If you do that shit even once, you'll dig yourself a hole you'll never get out of. It'll kill you eventually.'

'I know. But what if . . .'

'Shut up, Darlene. Just don't even think about it, OK?'

The party is over; eventually we realize that everyone else has disappeared and we are the only people left sitting at the kitchen table. We stumble out and make it home to bed in time for me to get one hour of sleep before I have to be at the Platter Palace.

Darlene has the day off, so I sneak out of the house, not waking her. Work is pure hell due to my idiotic behaviour the night before. Somehow I survive and on my return home I find a note from my partner in crime.

'Hello to the vagabond globetrotter. Wow. You have many blankets on your bed. It's like a big, soft womb in there. (What a stupid analogy, eh? As if I know what it's like to be in a womb!) I woke up sad today. I hope it goes away . . . The sight of the pizza box and the many condiments around it is giving me the urge to vomit. Perhaps I shall go do so. (Neatly and respectfully, of course.) Love and fluids, Darlene.'

She's called as well:

'Hey there sweet thing, it's me. I don't know if you've talked to Dick yet, but he did something for the local paper where he had to pick his five favourite new local bands and we are number four. That's right, Drool checks in at number four, which I think is good since we've practised twice and we don't have any songs and no one even knows who we are, so I think that's one of the greatest things I've ever heard. So we are number four and we should be practising tonight, don't you think? Even if Shan can't do it maybe you and I should take the evil substance and jam or whatever. Call me.'

We can never remember whose turn it is to bring beer to practice but none of us want to risk not having any, so we all three turn up with a twelve-pack of Black Label under our arms. Since each of us can easily polish off our own half case, this isn't a problem. Practice goes on for two hours longer than it was meant to; our beloved drummer goes upstairs to phone his girlfriend and sing 'me and the girls are still playing' to her over the phone. Darlene and I are on our backs on the dirty basement floor, surrounded by empty beer cans, broken strings and the crumbly cement eroding off the basement walls. We've been playing for so long that our hands and basses are covered in blood. Darlene is even sporting a huge gash on the side of her head caused by falling into the wall during a particularly boisterous version of 'Canister'. I still have my bass strapped on and I hit an open E which booms and echoes around our heads.

Darlene turns her head my way and says, 'Either I'm really fucked up or you're the best bass player I've ever heard in my life.'

We take turns hitting random strings and come to the conclusion that our band is hot shit. We are debating whether 'Aqueduct' or 'Iron Fireman' should be our first single when Shan comes bounding down the stairs. Darlene and I get up and start to brush cobwebs and crud off of each other.

'Look,' says Shan. We look down and see two grit angels, there on the filthy floor.

'Hi Claire, it's Darlene. Wait, that's not what I was going to say, I was going to say: Hi Suzette, it's Lucinda. I was just wondering what time we were going to go to the Grand Olde Opry. It's twelve fifteen and I'm waiting for you to call me. Dick called and he's on his way over from Lake and Chicago. Hopefully he'll get here alive. It's only two blocks. I don't know what's taking him so long. Anyway, we're gonna hang out and drink 3.2 beer and you're gonna call me and tell me where you're going, although, shit, where the hell could you be going at midnight. I mean, have you blown me off, Suzette? I'm not going to call you 'honey bunch' any more if you blow me off. That's it, love muffin, no more. So call me, it doesn't matter what time cause you know Lucinda leads a wild life. Bye.'

The word on the street was that we were fucking from day one, but it wasn't so. There were months of mental foreplay before the two of us figured out what everyone else knew all along and sex entered our picture. Unfortunately for me, our honeymoon didn't even have a chance to wear thin before my Dear Jane letter was tossed in my lap, citing all sorts of honourable reasons for ending things: the need to deal with the past once and for all, not being in the position to be the lover I deserve, blah blah blah. Despite feeling utterly like shit, I understood and even respected Darlene for knowing herself so well and facing her demons. Then two days later I discovered that she had fallen into bed with Buck, a man's man and arrogant fool who reckoned that since he could play guitar, he ruled the world.

I wouldn't mind so much being dumped for someone witty, intelligent and beautiful. But she ditched me for a shit like Buck.

'Hello CR, that's short for Claire Raylene if you couldn't figure that out. It's me. It's ten p.m. and you're probably upstairs in your little attic room. I drove by and the light was on and it looked really sweet. I'm at home now. I'm really really really bummed out and I wanted to see if you were awake and maybe I could come over and hang out with someone who likes me for real, you know, like a real friend, because there are so many people in this world who aren't real friends and it's really a drag. But you're asleep and it's selfish of me to even ask. Actually I feel better after talking to you this little bit, even if it is into your machine, I know you will listen to me. I hope you're not worrying about me too much. I think it's probably PMS mixed with the realization that the relationship that I'm in sucks. These two things together are sometimes hard to deal with so don't worry about me or anything. I'm going to go shoot heroin now. Ha ha. Talk to you later.'

It's best to be submerged in water when you feel like hell. We are buried in bubbles and candlelight.

'So what did Buck do now?' I ask, dreading having to comfort her over the man she dumped me for, but wanting it over with.

Darlene takes a deep breath. 'Well, I don't know how much of this is just me being mad at myself because I care so much, but I hate being made to feel as if I'm some sort of obligation or something. Maybe I'm expecting too much. He is a boy after all.'

'Darlene, having a penis doesn't exempt one from common courtesy. If he's acting like a jerk, you have every reason to be pissed off at him.'

'It just makes me so mad that he's forever giving me these excuses about why he didn't do such and such. Then when I call him on it, he accuses me of bitching at him. Why is it that whenever a woman stands up for herself, even in a calm and reasonable manner, she ends up being called a bitch? It's fucked. It's the sort of response you'd expect from someone who can't defend their behaviour so they try to turn it around and blame it on you. It comes down to the fact that if you don't give a flying fuck, you're just not going to do anything, right? So why make promises you have no intention of keeping? That's what I can't understand.'

I consider this for a while. 'I think Buck does care. But I also think that he's simply incapable of living up to his word. Maybe that's not his fault, but that doesn't mean you want to live with it.'

'Buck has some bizarre idea that because he's in a band, he has girls dropping at his feet and so he can treat me like shit. If he loses me, so what? There's plenty more to take my place.'

'Yeah, well, it could be that Buck's behaviour is caused by something far more complex and ugly than one man's shallow desire for rock stardom. It's out of his control. It has to be. No one would want to be such a shithead. If he could control it, he would.'

'The problem is, I love him.'

'At one point you may have seen something in him that made you love him, but I don't think it's there any more.'

'But what will I do if I lose him?'

'You're not losing shit. You're losing someone that you couldn't count on to piss on you if you were on fire,' I point out. 'You're not losing anything you're not better off without. He's the one losing something worth having, and he's too much of an idiot to know it.'

'I'm just mad at myself for caring so much.'

'Don't be. And don't feel like you were stupid about all this. You believed him because you're not someone who makes empty promises yourself. Your being involved with Buck at all, and your standing by him, says more about you than him.'

'I don't think I'll ever be able to trust anyone ever again.'

'For that I would like to skin him alive.'

'I don't know what I'm going to do. How the fuck am I going to live through this?'

'Completely Overloaded'

'Darlene, you must believe me, the day will come when you look back on this and wonder how you could feel so badly over someone so undeserving of you.' I splash water on Darlene's already wet face, and tell her: 'See, you're not crying. It's just me being obnoxious.'

She smiles a weak, wobbly smile, the first of the night, but it soon fades away. 'It just really pisses me off that I was always there for him and only now do I realize that he was never a friend to me at all.'

The water drips and the candles melt as Darlene cries herself to sleep, and I make sure she doesn't drown.

'Hello Suzette, this is Lucinda, your hopefully soon to be future house mate. I just need to tell you, I MUST tell you, that the more I think about this the more I think it's a fucking brilliant brilliant brilliant idea. I think we'd all be absolutely wonderful together and make good things happen all the time. I'm just totally excited about it and it's just fucking . . . I mean, of course we should live together. We should be already, it's just too obvious, you know. Call me.'

We did make good things happen all the time, for a while. Our Rock Room held our record collections and posters and a paperback copy of *'I'm with the Band'*. If there wasn't a show on that was the tiniest bit decent, people just turned up at our house and drank the night away. There were huge barbecues in the backyard; bands played in the basement. We had tons of fun – albeit unproductive fun.

It may be that we could have saved ourselves from the living hell our lives were about to become if only I hadn't started getting action with boys after years of only doing girls, and

Darlene hadn't freaked out as a result. But perhaps as intensely happy and connected as we were, it was inevitable that things would go bad. Horribly wrong.

There's no good to come of the telling of our tale of woe. Suffice to say that we hurt each other in ways that only two people who were as close as we were could. We cut each other to the bone and left ourselves to die, since neither of us could live without the other.

I went away to Australia to make a lifelong dream come true and returned, changed, a few weeks later. I found Darlene with a new band, home, lover; a life of her own without me in it. We licked our wounds, since we weren't ripping our scabs off on a daily basis any more, and secretly we were both relieved that the agony was over.

Months later, drunk on two measly beers, I stumble backstage at a Babes in Toyland show and there she is.

'Darlene, my love!'

'Claire, my sweet!'

Holding each other so tightly that we cannot breathe, we finally break away just enough to look at each other. We talk about Drool and the good old days with grins on our faces and tears in our eyes.

'I've missed you, Darlene,' I finally blurt out, unable to hold it in any longer. 'You know that, don't you?'

'Not as much as I've missed you. It's been so long that I can't even remember why we hate each other any more.'

'I never hated you, Darlene.'

'I know. You always loved me, no matter what.'

'I still do.'

'I love you too, CR.'

We stare into each other's eyes and smile. She breaks the silence. 'I should go.'

'Me too,' I answer.

'Bye, Suzette,' she whispers into my ear as she kisses me goodbye.

'Bye, Lucinda.'

She's not here any more, but Darlene comes down from the heavens to visit me now and again. Her words come out of a stranger's mouth and I look with shock for my beloved in a face that is not hers, wanting more than anything to reach out, grab her and convince her to stay. Or else, I'll be at a Cows show and an unseen hand will slip its way into mine. I'll turn to smile hello and find her grinning back at me.

As long as I live and breathe my partner in crime lives too, torn between here and there. When the day comes that I turn up at her place, Darlene will throw me the biggest party of all time, complete with freezer treats and the never-emptying fridge of beer.

Josie Kimber

'HAVING MYSELF A TIME'

He has left his bag in her room. A small black shoulder bag, not propped up against the eggshell wall, but close by; full and possibly heavy. Its frayed strap loops limply to one side, almost touching the leg of a wooden chair tucked under a table. The table might have looked across at this robust little bag and said, 'You can stand proud for now, but don't get too comfortable. This will never be your home. You've simply been forgotten.' And the bag, if it had bothered, might well have muttered, 'We'll see.'

The digital watch on the bedside unit beeps nineteen times to announce six minutes past one in the afternoon. When Eve bought the watch, she'd set it accurately. The alarm, however, refused to be shifted. Still, pragmatic as ever, she'd concluded that it was good for a girl to be aware of the time at least once a day. And today was to be a good day for time-keeping.

The lady wakes, slowly and elegantly, stretching. She reclines against the pink velour headboard, her breasts escaping a duvet stained from last month, last week and last night. Reaching past the watch for a bottle of vodka, she unscrews the lid, then gulps down three large mouthfuls. Hair of the dog, of course, but also a very pleasant way to wake up.

Her lips are dry and chapped and for the thousandth time she reminds herself to ditch that particular lipstick and buy one with all sorts of added lubricants. But she won't, because it took her three months to locate the perfect shade of red and she's damned if she'll attempt to live without it. So if she doesn't have soft

95

melting lips, then fine. Hers was not a mouth to be kissed softly. Running chipped red fingernails through tangled curly hair, she smiles. This is the smile of a girl who has been awake for a few minutes, but due to a hangover, has only just remembered.

The boy.

A pub in Brighton, in The Lanes. She'd arrived at half past eight to meet a friend at eight, bought herself a whisky and Coke, then sat down at a table meant for five. A long red dress was clinging to her body like a lover and her black-rimmed eyes might have warmed someone who couldn't get a seat near the fireplace. Sucking on a Marlboro, nicotine stained, overdressed and glorious, she saw him. He was sitting at the bar with a cigarette in one hand and a drink, probably vodka, in the other. Loosely curled around his neck was a black scarf and he wore a long black coat which looked well-cut and lived-in. He had auburn hair, a floppy fringe and several somethings about him. She stared shamelessly, as shameless staring was one of Eve's specialities and after all, everyone has to have a talent. Hmm, she thought, and, yes indeed. The boy looked like he'd stepped out of a Raymond Chandler novel.

She looked down at her drink, raised the glass, sipped and placed it back on the table, leaving a red smear on its rim. Red smears were a perennial thing with Eve. Other women left delicate traces of their perfume hanging in a room so as not to be forgotten, but Eve left smears. Smears on glasses, cups, cigarette butts and bodies. She was not a frail, breakable little thing and so a few droplets of fading scent would have been too swooning, too ladylike a reminder of where she'd been. Eve liked to leave evidence of what she'd done and she figured that some of the most important things she did were done with her mouth.

She tucked a ringlet behind her left ear and wondered when

he'd look at her. As he dragged on his cigarette, his eyes narrowed. She noticed the tip of his tongue sweeping over his bottom lip, then a slight tilt of the head in her direction. Their eyes locked for maybe three seconds before he looked down and smiled into his glass. It wasn't a confident smile, but then it wasn't shy either.

Well, this could be interesting, thought Eve.

He finished his drink rather quickly, caught the barman's attention, ordered the same again, stubbed out the cigarette and immediately lit another. Now, Eve was a girl with many turn-ons; that is to say she was generous in her scope and amenable to much, but there were about half a dozen things she couldn't say 'no' to. Chain-smoking rated highly. And so did a man who drank spirits instead of lager. This was a fairly practical preference, as in her experience, such men had better abdominal muscles. It also seemed to follow that they liked the right movies.

Inhaling with vigour never masked the damned. Eve had often thought, with regards to her own addiction, that she may not be the heaviest of smokers, but surely one of the most enthusiastic. Part-timers and those who muttered guiltily 'I must give up' after every cigarette should donate their rations to pure, upstanding patrons such as herself, she reasoned. It was important to get into the spirit of the thing. Smoking had thus far punctuated every significant moment of her life.

Without realizing, she'd already opened her Marlboro packet. Delicately she extracted another small friend and lit it with something approaching nostalgia. The clock on the wall read five to nine. Katie, though often late herself, may well have been and gone. Eve didn't mind this unreliability. She liked to picture her closest confidante in a whirl of satin and suitors; phonecalls and broken appointments. The fact that Katie wore an afghan coat and was often stoned in someone's bedsit had to be swept over for the sake of the friendship. Many was the time that Eve had turned a blind eye to an incense stick, or a crystal. Resigning herself to this unfortunate abandonment, the option of leaving didn't occur. There was drinking and looking to be done.

His eyes were with her as she stood. She disciplined the ringlet once more and slid hands over hips, adjusting the dress. In the pocket of her fake fur coat on the chair beside her she found some loose change: a few pound coins, tens and several twenties. Enough for another whisky and Coke, or perhaps this time a vodka. Slowly she prowled to the bar, impressing him with her lack of urgency.

Boldness is called for, Eve silently assured her nervous half. And so now she stood beside him, one hand on the bar, pale and small, aware that her gaze and his were on fortnight-old red nail varnish. A perfect summary of shared desires and pretensions: flaked varnish, dribbles of vodka in a small glass, a Zippo, some coins and a crumpled soft-pack of Marlboro. Clearly the important things in life, for both of them.

As they'd each cast themselves in a movie; daily getting in character for those precious seconds that turn to monochrome, what happened next would come as no surprise to anyone who's watched *Casablanca* or *Brief Encounter* late at night, alone. Eve scooped up her money as the boy reached for his Zippo. Obviously, their hands had to brush ever so slightly, their eyes had to meet – heads turning with equally measured languor – and without a doubt, they had to speak.

'Sorry,' he said.

'No problem.'

Recompense for the hangover is the cinematic haze, almost as if to say, 'Well, yes, you are going to throb and ache, you do have to suffer and pay, but here, have some beautifully edited highlights of the night before to make it worthwhile, to make you do it all again.' Eve places the empty vodka bottle back on the unit. Lighting the first cigarette of the day, she leans back, closes her eyes and indulges. She's remembered the building up of sexual tension, she's going to skip fumbled conversation and move straight to her bedsit, last night, messing around and getting it on and, this part, she's going to play, rewind, pause and play for at least half an hour.

His name was Robert, he was a music journalist and he'd taken off his scarf and coat. He sat on her bed, pretty drunk and decently nervous, while she unbuckled her black patent shoes. Rubbing the instep of her left foot, she looked up and suggested,

'Vodka?'

'Cheers.'

She passed him the bottle, thinking how damn fine his mouth looked around it.

'Shall I put some tunes on?'

'Yeah, that'd be good,' he answered, with a voice that suitably matched his hair, the coat he'd removed and the manner in which he smoked.

She padded over to the tape deck and casually pressed 'play', knowing full well that Billie Holiday was ready to assist the seduction. A seduction of the best kind, the sort where you've been guaranteed success, so you can stop worrying about that and concentrate on the execution.

She returned to the bed slowly; heavy-lidded by design. He was going to kiss her, or she was going to kiss him, and although it didn't really matter who initiated it, she fully approved when he did. It got matters off to a good start. His lips were gentle, his tongue tentative, but soon and luckily, this changed. She felt his hands becoming less reverent, as garments that could have been skilfully slipped off were pulled at; the strain of a seam being a beautiful thing.

At one point: his mouth on her nipple and two fingers inside her, she didn't think, here I am again. What she did think, randomly and repeatedly, was, yes, oh Christ, more, harder and come here. If he stopped now, if he took those fingers away, she was going to die, no question.

He lifted his head from her breast and started licking her neck. Her nails on his back sank deep into skin as he whispered,

'I like it when you hurt me a little.'

Enough was enough. She had to feel his cock in her mouth. She wanted to taste it; to claim it. She pushed him roughly away and went down. Her curls tickled his stomach; his hands in her curls. He lifted his pelvis to meet the last remnants of red which stained her mouth, Eve's mouth and not any mouth, sliding over and up again, down and then up.

Maybe it was the memory of the way he'd drunk his vodka, or the intimate circling of lips around endless cigarettes; possibly the way he'd fingered her, that is, very well (unlike so many young men before him), or the firmness of his stomach and the demons caught on his retina, but as she moved faster, she thought,

I'll come. He doesn't have to do anything. I'll just come.

Followed by the raising of her head and the words,

'Fuck me.'

Well, what's a boy to do?

As she took him inside, he told her how beautiful she was. Boys say this, they say this to Eve quite often. Maybe it was true, or maybe it was something that boys just said, like the apology you give to someone who collides with you in the street. A 'good form' affair; the mark of a gent. Although, the way he kissed her face whilst holding her close and himself back, made her think he might have meant it.

Almost there, then, her breasts against his chest, his hair brushing her cheek, she squeezed this man tight; she sucked him in. Muffled by pockets of hot breath, she stammered,

'I'm-going-to-come.'

Fucking hell, yeah. The neighbours would have something to talk about, bless them. He let himself go seconds later, aggressive; vulnerable.

Afterwards, wrapped up in each other, they forgot about post-coital smoking for the longest time.

Dwelling on this, the tender way he'd held her, Eve stubs out the cigarette and throws the duvet aside. She looks down at her milky skin, all curves and man-traps, and thinks that her body had begun, of late, to feel like public property. For some reason, Robert has not left her considering it common ground. Rather, she feels like a cat with its head in a bucket of cream.

Her fingers play kiss-chase round her nipples as she gets out of bed. She walks over to the chair and picks up a red fake silk dressing gown, pulls it on, yawns, then proceeds to make coffee. The room smells like an ashtray made of vodka, aftershave and sex, which is just the way she likes it. Bringing herself and her caffeine back to the chair, she remembers waking up in the night, tingling and rippling with the boy's head between her thighs, his tongue moving rapidly over her clitoris, then slightly inside her. She'd come against his face almost instantly. You see, she was the kind of girl that men did things to, some things stranger than others, but no one had ever woken her up by going down. Such a simple act, really; so obvious, but this boy – this floppy-fringed

101

stranger – had been the first. When he emerged from under the duvet, she'd held him tightly to her and they'd talked the room out of darkness.

Oh my God, she grins, wider awake by the second. He wants to see her again. He'd got up at about ten to ten, scrambled around for clothes, then kissed all of her face, sweetly. A date had been fixed, for nine o'clock this evening at, at – they were to meet at – *where?*

Oh, Christ. Oh, no. Think, think. Slow, deep breaths.

Eve is pacing the room now, her head in her hands. She is almost shaking. This can't be happening. All those previous boys, some of whom had wanted to meet up: she'd had no difficulty with times and places then. And the rotten thing was that through years of well-trained apathy, she hadn't cared. But now she did. This one was special.

Instinctively, she grabs a cigarette and destroys it quickly, thinking,

It's my own fault. I should have been more awake. I should have repeated back to him where we're meant to meet. Oh, I just shouldn't have let him go. I should have given him a blow-job to make him stay. Why didn't I do that?

Eve's pragmatism appears to have abandoned her. She stops dead in the centre of the room, trying to relocate it.

Oh, come on, he's probably not going to turn up anyway. He'll get home, shower, type up an article about some minor Brighton indie band, then go to the pub with his mates. He'll spend the whole evening telling them about this girl he pulled and they'll all laugh, like boys do. I hate boys.

She throws her shoulders back resolutely and straightens the bed, aware that he's not going to boast to his friends, that he's not the kind, but hey, he probably won't turn up for some other, less laddish reason. Then she remembers him looking back, halfway through the door, and saying,

'You will turn up, won't you?'

'Of course I will,' she'd replied.

'Good. See you at nine, then.' A beautiful smile and, 'Bye.'

'Bye.'

Oh shit. He was going to be there, wasn't he, just to spite her, just to prove himself the perfect fucking boy she already thought he was.

Right then, pull it together, she tells herself sternly. Relax. Have a shower. Do the washing-up. Go for a ten mile run.

She was unable to relax, she loathed washing-up and she intended to spend the rest of her life not going for ten mile runs. She would have a shower, that's what she'd do. Yes. Opening the door of the bedside unit, she extracts a soap dish, shampoo and conditioner. Hanging on the back of the door is a large green towel, which she flings over her shoulder, toiletries nestled between breasts and arms.

Although hot water soothes aching muscles, Eve feels a twinge of regret as the soap runs over her body. This ritual cleansing business is not particularly welcome today. She's washing away the scent of him and the invisible marks his fingers made on her skin.

Ten minutes later, she's sitting on the edge of the bed feeling wretched. And then she sees it.

He has left his bag in her room.

'Oh, you've finally been noticed,' mumbles the table.

His bag. In her room. She rushes forward, falls to her knees and embraces it as though it were him. This is his bag; he takes it everywhere, she thinks. Suddenly she draws back.

What am I doing? Why is this boy so important?

If her mind hasn't yet grasped it, her body understands. She lifts the bag up and presses it to her chest.

I don't care, she thinks. I want him. I'll just look inside for a wallet, or diary. There might be a phone number. I can ring him, apologize and find out where we're meeting. OK, he might be a little hurt that I've forgotten, but he'll know how tired I was. And I'll explain that I had to look in his bag to get the number. He'll understand.

The notion that this innocuous bundle might contain private items he wouldn't want her to see is descending like a fine summer shower. It would seem to be a good time to make more coffee and smoke another cigarette.

She places the bag gently on the floor, exactly where she'd found it, switches on the kettle and disrobes. Standing naked by the sink, she recalls the warmth of his body in abandon; the angles and abdominals which she'd kept safe. Two bits of white trash in a cheap bedsit, on that cheap bed, but together soaring past all this, past Brighton.

The kettle boils as she climbs into thick black tights and a short black dress. She grabs the coffee mug from the table, heads back towards the kettle and——

The Blue Parrot. Nine o'clock at The Blue Parrot.

There is a God, then; a God that understands about cheap women and romance. Restraining the urge to run out of the room and make friends with all her mean and prudish neighbours, she allows herself a face-cracking grin and a large yelp. This flash of memory, proof that her brain is not yet pickled past the point of no return, must be duly honoured with extra coats of mascara and lipstick.

Eve is now a very happy woman. Her coffee tastes better and her Marlboro lasts longer. Lovingly, she opens her make-up bag, scatters cosmetics across the bed and begins to put on her face. Pale foundation and a sweep of translucent loose powder. Creamy white eye shadow, lots of black eyeliner and three coats of lash lengthening, soul-uplifting black mascara. All these to be followed by a perfect application of the reddest of red lipsticks – true red and bloody – Eve's red. All made-up with somewhere to go.

It is half past two: all essential tasks completed. Madam is ready to face the world, should she so desire. Is there anything worth facing out there today, before nine o'clock? Maybe she should go to Boots just before closing and spray on some expensive perfume; some Chanel No 5, perhaps, then wiggle along the beach like Marilyn Monroe. Or, possibly, she could ring Katie to suggest meeting up for coffee. No. Eve wants to be alone until she sees Robert again. She doesn't want to waste precious conversation on anyone else. She should spend the rest of the day thinking up disarming comments to tinkle in his direction.

She wanders over to the tape deck, consigns Billie Holiday to the shelf and puts on *Rattlesnakes* by Lloyd Cole and The Commotions. The small black bag catches her eye. She moves towards it, bends down and rests on her heels, a wave of indecision taking its place beside her happiness. There is no need to look inside. She's remembered where they're meeting, so any acquaintanceship between the bag and herself need only be short and formal.

You're going to ignore this bag, she instructs herself, until ten minutes to nine; at which point you'll put on your coat and gloves, check that your keys are in your pocket for the fifth time, then nonchalantly pick it up, sling it over your shoulder, take it to The Blue Parrot and return it to him. If you do this, you'll be able to smile the smile of the honest whilst staring him straight in the eye.

She doesn't move away. Her fingertips fondle the shoulder strap. What's inside? It's so full. It must be full of special things. Such a special boy, so well-dressed and elegant, so beautifully accessorized; a boy who conveys glamour and decadence in the swish of his coat, with a wave of the hand. A boy like this would probably have plane tickets to New York and *American Psycho*, inscribed. And what else? Things so wonderfully him; magnificent; supreme; she can't begin to imagine. These precious belongings will validate all her expectations and fill her with joy. She has to look. She can't.

The strap falls back to the floor as Eve marches over to the cupboard by the sink. She pulls out a biscuit tin designated for bill money. Inside she finds two five pound notes. Biting her bottom lip, she folds them in her hand, carries them to the table and puts them in her purse. She'd already decided to take a fiver to buy drinks, but this second note is more significant. She knows full well that at ten minutes to nine she won't be putting on her coat in an orderly fashion. Instead, she'll be reapplying lipstick and changing her outfit for the fourth or fifth time. In short, she'll be late to meet him, and although she never really means to be late for anyone, she just is. It's more than a bad habit now, it's a muscle-memory affair. Her body just can't be on time. So: this money will pay for a taxi. Robert warranted punctuality. Bugger the electricity meter.

This decided, she turns once again to the bag. She ponders the morality of opening it. No one will see; no one will know. Does she need to adhere to strict ethical codes while alone in her bedsit?

Fuck it. She unfastens the clasp clumsily, with the enthusiasm of a kid smoking in the school toilets. Tipping the enigma upside down, she empties its contents on to the floor.

A cheap, shabby wallet; a condom; a cheque book; the demo tape of a band she's never heard of; a pad; a Biro; an unopened packet of Marlboro and a bulky, black jumper.

A few minutes pass before Eve puts these things carefully back into the bag. She stands up, gets her purse, removes the second five pound note and returns it to the biscuit tin. She sits on her bed and lights a cigarette. Then she smiles. How perfectly right and marvellous. He keeps ordinary stuff in his bag, like she does. Their glamour was worn on the outside, on display. That was the point.

She relaxes completely, knowing that she could be late, as always; that he would want her to be.

Jenny Knight

'SCHERING PC4 –
A LOVE STORY'

I'm sitting in a green chair in the ladies' waiting room at Riverside Sexual Health Clinic. In front of me are ladies' magazines. All around me are forlorn looking ladies. I smile pleasantly, but they stare at their shoes. I examine the leaflets on the wall.

HERPES SIMPLEX TYPE 2: Recurrent virus infection. Water-filled blisters that may crust over or become ulcers, located on or near the genitals. First infection is usually intensely painful, particularly for women. No known cure or effective treatment.

'*Ohhh*,' the nurses sigh in unison. I put my chin to my chest and stare down between my legs with them. They shake their heads and murmur in empathy. It has taken me a long, long time to walk here, with care, and I am grateful for the sympathy. I make sorry little whimpers as Doctor pokes around, and the nurses say 'there, there'. I notice that one of them has Nordic features, and wonder if she is one of those Finnish nurses that are supposed to be rampaging around our wards. I am about to ask when Doctor harshly scrapes a sample from one of my blushing blisters without warning.

'*Ohhh!*' he says, before I can so much as squeak. '*Ohhh*, that must have hurt.' I turn my head aside in suffering.

'Ouch,' I whisper. He delves back in again.

'Just another leetle . . . *ohhhh!*' The Nordic nurse pats my quivering thigh. I exit with a limp and strict instructions to take a salty bath.

111

Jenny Knight

CHLAMYDIA. Most common sexual infection in the western world. In females, symptoms include inflammation, swollen glands and prolonged bleeding.

I've come off the Pill because I've been bleeding heavily and mysteriously for the last three weeks. I've come to Riverside because Max is starting to get very annoyed, and is whining and scratching at my pants every bed-time. I have my pastel blue pants on today, in the examining room, and I'm rather embarrassed that one of the blonde nurses might catch sight of them, so I tuck them into my discarded jeans, being careful to fold them over and around the unsightly stain. The paper towelling is scratchy beneath my back, and crumples as I fidget my legs into the stirrups. 'Slide forward a leetle,' breathes Doctor. I edge my bottom towards him. 'More, more,' he says impatiently. I bounce closer. 'That's eet.' The three of them peer inwards. Doctor blows his nose. 'Hmm,' Doctor says, and the nurses nod. It's chilly in here. Doctor gives me a Schering PC4 pack to take care of any nasty little pregnancies, and two whole bottles of pills just for me. I am tickled pink.

SCHERING PC4 is the faithful Morning After Pill — a girl's best friend. That description is actually inaccurate. Not many people know this, but it can be taken up to 72 hours after intercourse. I know.

Tonight we make love again. I am worried it is taking too long and he will be frustrated. I frantically thrust my hips and make frightened-little-kitten noises at each of his clenched-teeth lunges, like: *enh! enh!* I'm sure you have your own noise. At last, with a tremendous effort, Max expels his precious bodily fluids into my . . . into me, and collapses on top of me, all red

112

and wet like a new-born baby. I kiss his sweaty neck and pat his back. There, there. Well done. Thank you. Max bounces up and across the room, humming. I lie still. I feel repulsed; proud; wet. It's curious. I try a smile. I don't want to appear ungrateful.

'Wine, my love?' asks Max.

'*You will be seek,*' Doctor's words ring jovially in my ear.

Max smiles and tilts his head to one side in that way he does. I am weak.

Certain antibiotics, such as metronidazole and co-amoxyclav, can be particularly poisonous in combination with alcohol, and may induce vomiting.

I am sickety-sick-sick.

Swimming in front of me are two mushrooms, pirouetting in a coy courting ritual. They are soon encircled by twirling skirts of broccoli florets in froth, and then dark, dangerous beef chunks, pouncing on top of them, dunking them under. I am spell-bound.

'You look run-down,' Max says through a mouth of Colgate, all concerned. Max says I am highly strung and neurotic, but that's why I'm his little princess.

'I can help you, darling,' Max says, taking my little face in his hands. 'I will.'

I say nothing. For my mouth is full.

SYPHILIS is a highly contagious, complicated disease. It can persist for years and cause serious, life-threatening damage, including severe disability with damage to the heart and blood vessels and the nervous system. It can be treated in the first instance with penicillin and, if this fails, docycycline hydrochloride or acrosoxacin can be used.

Jenny Knight

I am almost reluctant to put aside the copy of *Madam* I am reading, as I am in the middle of an intriguing article on 'The G Spot: Myth or *Mmmmmm*?', but Doctor beckons me into the Room with a brusque greeting. I give him a wink to show I'm not at all flustered, and delicately arch my insteps into the rough canvas. A young medical student with an optimistic moustache is invited to prod my glands, and I am pleased I had the foresight to shave my bikini line. He pushes them around my groin a little, and hmms and haws uncertainly. 'A first class case of syphilis!' Doctor tells him, and he looks relieved. A swab of yellow goo is extracted and admired, before being filed away carefully some place behind my head. 'Wonderful!' says Doctor, and they walk away, apparently forgetting me.

I am positioned alluringly across the rumpled royal blue sheets, which are flecked with satisfied semen. Max is in the marble green bathroom. I can hear him making his manly noises. I hear a forlorn honk of the nose, a hawk of the throat, a 'phoo-ee' and an 'ahh!' He emerges, shrouded casually in a large fluffy towel, and followed by a cloud of Calvin Klein. 'Okay, my princess?' he puckers. That's his pet-name for me. We smile indulgently at each other. As he disrobes once more, I stealthily slide the crumpled toilet paper from between my legs and down the side of the mattress, making a mental note to take it to Riverside later. I raise my arm. 'Darling!' I say.

CHLAMYDIA: If not caught in time can cause complications in pregnancy. The male carrier is often unaware of the infection. Failing to treat the male partner can result in the reinfection of the woman.

Previous partners . . . last period . . . blah, blah, blah. At the other end of my legs I can see my socks are slightly blackened

114

from my shoes. I wiggle one big toe. Wiggle the other. I watch Doctor's furrowed brow between my thighs with detached interest. I suddenly feel strangely maternal. I wonder if he's discovered anything exciting. I have an annoying habit of trying to suggest to doctors the diagnosis. I know it. It makes it more fun for me, though, and I'm only trying to help.

'Chlamydia!' smirks Doctor, rubbing his hands. I was going to say that. Chla-myd-i-a. It's rather pretty. I picture a troop of white corpuscles rushing to the scene of the crime.

'You and her are like old friends!' he guffaws with a careless flourish of his spatula. The Finnish nurse is not so nice this time, and must have removed at least three layers of my sinful cervix during her scraping.

Back in the corridor, Doctor takes the seat next to mine. Hands me my Schering PC4. 'Your womb is a haven for parasites!' Doctor chuckles. My hands instinctively fly to cocoon my belly. I am miserable. There is an aching in my heart and a burning in my uterus. I pick at my mouth in shame. A bit comes off. Doctor doesn't appear to notice, and continues:

'You are attractive to men, I understand,' he says. True enough. I adhere the bit to my skirt. 'But—'

'But you are not a careful young lady.' He is beaming at me.

'But I love him,' I say, all weepy.

'Who?' says Doctor, suddenly interested.

'*Him*.' I am overcome with weeps.

'Him who? There are many hims, yes?'

I'm staring at a copy of *Hussy*. Patsy Kensit is on the cover.

'You do not get the entire back catalogue of Venereal Diseases without a little help from your friends. Heh heh heh heh heh!'

This is impossible, of course. I'm a good girl, I am. 'But there's only Max,' I protest, mooningly.

'Then Max is a bad boy!' laughs Doctor. Laughing at me.

My glands swell in indignation. I picture Max's determined little spermatozoa swimming bravely for my fallopian tubes, without even an orgasm to help them on their merry way.

'I don't expect to see you in here again, young lady!' Doctor waggles his finger.

I picture them trickling cheerily down my crevices, gathering plasma-like on the sheet. Doctor loads me up with Durex and steers me to the door.

I am sickety-sick-sick.

I'm sitting very still on the top deck of the 73. Stoke Newington whisks past. I'm not pleased. I think carefully. I knew it wouldn't last with Max, of course. I knew I'd spoil it somehow. The original plan had been to eventually snap tight as a spring in his face, without warning, without reason, without a doubt. I would become all tired and emotional after some long night's drinking, and alarm him with my crazy-lady insecurity: clinging like a limpet to his arm, throwing him sorrowful, baleful looks over his pint, listlessly trailing him from pub to pub, and bursting into tears in front of his friends. O Max, Max! And then, when I'd hounded him home through sheer embarrassment and rage, I would crumple up my face in ugly hysteria, mash my sodden nose against his shirt, and beat my wobbly girl fists against his cruel, unforgiving frame; until we were way past the point of no return and floundering in the messy swamps of female neuroses. O woe, woe! However, this new development calls for an entirely different plan of action. Not slashing suits. Not slashing myself. But slashing away all the unpleasantness. Max is contaminated. Max is unclean. Max must be cleansed.

'Schering PC4 — A Love Story'

A swab is taken by pushing a loop on a big plastic stick into the ur-eth-ra at the tip of the penis, all helpless and naked like a baby bird and contracting in fear. This really hurts. To take a specimen for a viral culture, a cotton bud is poked into the lesion and wiggled around for a bit. This really hurts too. A negative culture does not necessarily mean that the patient is not infected. The test should be taken again until the nurse is convinced of the accuracy of the results. Again 'n' again 'n' again. Until Nursey is quite satisfied, and Patient is quite repentant. And then again for luck.

Love hurts, darling.
Hurts when you pee.

Amy Lamé

'MAPPING'

Joyce was Priss' aunt, the youngest sister of her dead mother. Priss had arrived at Joyce's four years ago when she was ten and didn't even know where Brazil was. A product of the sexual revolution in the early seventies, Joyce was the kind of aunt every girl wants, and every girl wants to be. She smoked long cigarettes. Bought Priss peach flavoured lip gloss. Permed her own hair. And refused to let Priss call her 'aunt', which made her all the more alluring.

Priss spun the globe round and round like an out-of-control hula hoop, shutting her eyes tight as venus flytraps fresh from the kill. Her fingertips skimmed the surface, reading the mountains and rivers. Priscilla mouthed the names quietly to herself . . . Alps, Atlantic, Appalachian, ready to stop at a destination unfamiliar to her remaining four senses.

After-school afternoons slipped by in dreams of an Africa so black it seemed a glowing purple, desert homes swirling with sand, each drop of water more precious than platinum, and guarded intently by an unsmiling noble tribesman. Priss (as Joyce called her), didn't know this for sure, but it seemed likely. After all, she knew Africa was full of deserts. Deserts are parched dry. And almost everyone from Africa is black. So Priss spun stories like variegated yarn, pieced together with strands of information she gleaned from her globe and a musty 1973 edition of *Encyclopaedia Britannica*.

Priss often couldn't see anything but lines, borders, creeks, public land demarcations, latitude and longitude. Even the dinners Joyce haphazardly prepared for her each night became topographical and geographical. Reconstituted mashed potatoes formed the Pennine hills, with a puddle of gravy nestling in the Ribble Valley. The fried pork cutlet possessed an uncanny resemblance to China, with a streak of gristle winding through it imitating the Great Wall. Priscilla imagined her helping of sweetcorn to be the Thousand Islands in Canada, all piled on top of each other after an imaginary ill-natured tornado. She couldn't wait to see what the pudding would look like.

'Oh girl, just eat it 'stead-a starin' at it like ya was lookin' for a tick on a spotted dog!' Joyce said tartly, her mules clicking and sticking on the linoleum tiled floor. Priss could usually smell Joyce's lacquered hair and White Shoulders eau de toilette wafting yards ahead of Joyce's arrival into any room. But while Priss was following the Rochdale Canal moving into the Yellow River, not even Joyce's lethargic click-clack walk and omnipresent odour could have broken her concentration.

Without responding, Priss gulped her dinner in the time it would have taken a tsunami to destroy Bangladesh. She watched Joyce slyly out of the corner of her eye. Joyce's behind was big.

'I may have a big butt,' Joyce would say, 'but I could wrap an Italian salami around my waist without *any* problem!' It was hot, and her pendulous breasts were encased in a wisp of a lycra tube, nipples ever closer to her navel. Chunky rolls of flesh peeked out above the waistband of her shorts, her panty line showing through the white cotton. She chewed Dentyne, snapping it like an elastic band on the back of an unsuspecting neck.

As Priss scraped the last few islands from her plate, she traced the knots of veins on Joyce's legs, snarled like a Tokyo traffic jam. She had seen motorways and spaghetti junctions swelling since she sat down at the kitchen table. Her legs were throbbing like the Mississippi ready to flood the Bible Belt

'Ain't no dessert tonight, Priss. Growin' girls like you should be watchin' yer figure.' Priss was aware of her expanding flesh, and to her it was a great uncharted territory. But Joyce was trying to fence in Priss' outward expansion. Priss knew big countries were taken seriously. After all, who pays attention to Liechtenstein? A bellyful of Lancashire, Canadian and Chinese could not satiate Priss' hunger. She was a growing girl, and girls need nourishment with a capital N.

She left her empty plate on the table, went to her room, and spun her globe. Her finger landed on Egypt. Priss kept a stash of biscuits and sweets under her bed for the nights when Joyce wouldn't let her have pudding. She reached for the tin under her bed and opened it. She unfolded her map of Africa and traced the Nile River from Lake Nasser in the south to the tippy-top branches north of Cairo.

'Egypt,' she repeated over and over, savouring the two syllables, split and nourished by the Nile. She wondered what Nile water tasted like . . . silt or salt? Balanced on the Tropic of Cancer, the sun tingled on her pale skin. Voices of Egyptian goddesses with varicose veins whispered in her ear at the point where the Mediterranean and Red Seas collide. She munched a biscuit and brushed crumbs from her thighs. She felt her growing hips and sensed her skin stretching to accommodate her appetite. Her heart was thumping fast, her tender breasts expanding as she felt the Nile rising in her belly. Grasping the map, she pressed it to her forehead and inhaled the scent of papyrus and ink. Her breath quickened. Plump fingers trekked over pyramids, valleys and plateaus to reach a moist and salty river. She grabbed a biscuit, found her delta and sensed the tremors of a tidal surge. The dam broke and she fell asleep with her knickers around her ankles, a map of Egypt covering her face, and a Jaffa cake in her vagina.

Helen Mead

'WEDNESDAY NIGHT, THURSDAY MORNING'

WE KISSED for the last time, that night. And when I woke the next morning, you were gone. The sofa-bed looked, as always, like it couldn't wait to reassemble itself: crumpled under the weight of a night's sleep. Covered minimally by its pink, seventies bedsheet with elastic corners that fought you while you tried to pin them down and won while you were asleep. We'd spent a lot of time on this sofa-bed over the last year, me and Jenks. Ever since our birth into acid house we'd invested the majority of our coming-down time here, in this living room – dancing, smoking, talking, sleeping. It was Ross and Debs' flat – we'd met through our love of music and/or (depending on your perspective) our mutual and perpetual pursuit of good times. I remember those late nights and early mornings so clearly, like nothing else (literally) – most other memories, Christmas and Guy Fawkes night (the first time Luce ventured up to London on her own for a night out with her big sister), have been obliterated, judged by my memory not to be worth the ram they're stored on. This is what was important to remember . . .

IT WOULD usually be daylight before we returned home to more music, more drugs. Different drugs. In all the time I knew him, Ross never bothered to learn to skin up. Jude always did it. King size. One-skinners. Such intense concentration and total absorption in the face above the busy fingers in the early morning light as we drank tea and started, probably for the first time since we'd come together for the night, to chat and to chill.

There's nothing better than getting home with the sunrise. Days lapping themselves. Going on forever. It was greedy, this love. Our soundtracks were self-perpetuating and our love of them seemingly inexhaustible. Wherever you went you heard little pockets of London plugged-in to the sound. The ethic. The Victorian back streets of Kensal Rise where Ross and Jude's top floor flat nestled in a row of terraces may have been a fair old ride from downtown Detroit but when we returned tripping and Inner City's 'Good Times' greeted us from the homecoming tape collection we felt we had neighbours all across the globe. It was more than reassuring, it was lifting, affirming, confirming what we already sensed but had no physical proof of – that we were part of a universal language that traversed oceans. We were connected. We knew our generation was unstoppable. And *this* was the way.

We were silly. We were carefree. There was always, always something to celebrate. Life was for living. We knew that now. And it was good. So good. Pleasure came from anything and everything. We could scare ourselves stupid with *Pee Wee's Big Adventure*, rewinding and rewinding the scary moment where the truck driver's red, spiral eyes bug-out on springs, until the tape was permanently scarred and we were on the floor giggling. We'd eat lime-green milk jelly with hundreds-and-thousands for our regressive birthday bashes, washed down with pink cham-pagne and a free E from our dealer to celebrate the occasion (we must have been good customers). We'd gather there for Carnival, listening to Northern Soul tapes a friend brought over. We'd even concede to turn up the volume on *Hitman And Her* when Technotronic's 'Pump Up The Jam' came on, even if it was the epitome of cheese. We didn't care. It was time to feel like a child again, to not know fear, self-consciousness, or responsibilities. It was time to have fun. As long – and for as long – as you could still get to work on time.

THAT'S WHY I'd done the sensible thing that week. I'd taken the day off. It seemed like the only thing to do. It was a Wednesday night and the last night of Shoom: I didn't want to risk having to go to work feeling that happy next day. Somebody might think there was something wrong.

Shoom was our favourite club. It had been all summer. 'Shoom', it was said, was the sound the records made as Danny selected the next up and waved it above his head like a fast-rising and ever-quicker setting sun eclipsing above him. Of course it wasn't a sound you could ever have heard – we were in a nightclub, for Christsakes! It was more a sound you could see: 'Shooom!-Shoooom!-Shoom!-Shooom!' As the edge of the vinyl cut deftly through the air, the ecstasy in our pupils providing us with an audible hallucination to accompany the buzz. Seeing was literally believing. Altered states, always altered states. But the same altered state. Ecstasy. Each week it was like being Mr Ben, walking through the back of the clothes shop and each time returning to the same paradise: suspended in its own reality, like nothing could change it . . . even time. We were all regulars there. We all knew each other, even if we didn't know each others' names. And our lives seemed to cross everywhere, even in a city as big as London.

Suddenly we had a whole new network of friends. People we might have never met before. There was the dark-haired Latin senorita from Café Paradiso in Covent Garden who bumped us to the front of the queue because she recognized our faces from the dancefloor; the bubbly blonde bob-headed girl at the sandwich bar opposite work who'd leave the club and go straight in to prepare her fillings until our still-dilated, happy and knowing pupils would meet over a brie and walnut sandwich at about two the next afternoon, when I got a late lunch and she was thinking about getting home; then there was the guy I recognized once I'd already got into the dentist's chair – actually he did a good job and the music was still the coolest I've heard, house's mutoid acid squelches tripped out further to the timing of the drill. There were hundreds of regulars and we'd check each other wherever we went – town or country, but usually somewhere Danny or Andy were playing. You could always tell a Shoom regular: we always let off to the same tunes. Threw our hands in the air and our bodies more lucidly, more passionately, into the rhythm when they dropped our specific, particular calls to the dancefloor – Cry Sisco's 'Afrodisiac' with its jungle-bird call and a Humphrey Bogart sample from *The African Queen* or Danny's remix of Illusion's mid-eighties cut of Timmy Thomas' 'Why Can't We Live Together?'

It still raises the fur on my goosebumps, as it did beneath the dry ice when I trip back to that time. I remember one time: a special time, down the Valbonne on a sunny (even inside) Sunday afternoon, when the club owner wouldn't let us have: 'Just *one* more!' We were persistent. No-one would leave. Our communion wasn't yet over. We wouldn't accept it. (I told you our love was greedy, sometimes insatiable.) We were demanding. We wouldn't let it rest until we got our own way. The pressure was incredible, so purely charged, motivated by nothing other – in reality – than our need to feel that bond run through us some more, to have one last respite before the umbilical cord was cut again until the next time; our next rapture . . . The crowd had formed a semi circle radiating back from the DJ booth, everybody was calling, clapping, whistling, pumping the vibe: 'One more!' . . . Coke high. Higher and higher. Never gonna stop. No limits . . . Then the energy took a physical form with clarity. As an angel of a girl in a brown fur bra with the greenest eyes I'd ever seen, broke the circle with her unamplified voice. Silence. Still. She opened her mouth and sang: 'Why Can't We Live Together?' It came on so strong. Every piece of energy in that place drawn up into her lungs and into our hearts. They stopped, on the down beat, as we marvelled. It was what we'd needed. A piece of magic. Some sign that made us feel so, so good inside. After, when we drove home, back past the venue, we saw her standing inside the driver's side door, towelling herself dry and changing into a warm cable-knit sweater. Sensible clothing. And took out her contact lenses and swapped them for little, neat, square metal-rimmed glasses. It was the first time I'd seen coloured contact lenses.

THAT WEDNESDAY night, I went to Shoom with my girlfriend Andy (Andrea in her original north-east incarnation). Well not so much 'went' as 'came.' She was a pill baby too. Delighting in finding new people to drop the magic pill on, like some seductress priestess. First balancing it between their tongue and conscience, and progressing slowly. Be there for their subconscious when they came up. As much a pleasure to administer as to experience. Maybe more. A passing-on of wisdom as profoundly wordless as only psycho-spiritual experiences can be. Taking your first E is a ritual: a bit like – no, totally like – losing your virginity; you want it to be with someone who shares the knowledge with pleasure. Treasure. Ecstasy is to covet. To lose yourself in.

Ross and Nona were my E parents. I hadn't thought about trying it at all before. It wasn't an option. The two times Jenks

131

checked it, I ended up sitting outside the UCH Accident and Emergency department with him in the passenger seat of my electric blue Beetle for hours, convinced he was about to have a heart attack. And I'd been spiked with acid at thirteen; nearly got myself killed walking backwards into the street, in front of a car. It had sort of put me off the idea of further fourth-dimension experiences. I didn't like the idea of drugs. I hadn't enjoyed the loss of control.

It was Spring. I'd gone over to some friends' new offices after work and a few of us went for the first drinks of the season in a pub garden by the river. At closing time Ross, Steve and Nona decided to go to a club. I went too. I was having fun. Too much to stop. Nona put half a pill in my mouth while we were in the car on the way to Camden, lost in the maze of one-way streets in the city. It tasted bitter and there was nothing to wash it down with, except saliva. By the time we arrived at High On Hope, I'd already entered that world where you bounce when you walk, laugh when you talk and smile because it's good to be happy. By the time the chorus of Chaka Khan's 'I'm Every Woman' had repeated itself for the last time I was very pleased with my new friends. I'd bonded with my new soul mates.

I got home at four a.m. and never felt so good, after so little sleep, as I did that next morning. Body caressed by my bath in a state of ultra-aliveness. Work a breeze. It was Friday and I couldn't wait for the weekend. Steve had invited me to another party that night. A secret party. A house party. I'd know other people: Ross and Jude would be there. Jenks and Andy could come to . . . That's where they were turned on. And that's where it all started: dancing in the shingle on the balcony outside under the stars. The beginning of our discovery.

* * *

'Wednesday Night, Thursday Morning'

SOMETIMES, like I planned tonight, I would stay at Andy's place in Stepney Green. Girls' world. Escape. I felt safe there. It looked like Ripper territory when the fog hit the streets. It kind of scared me, in a silly, unreal way, like a nightmare that recurs so often it starts influencing your life. So that you gripped the sharp-edged keys between the clenched fingers that make a fist in your fleece-lined, hooded-jacket pocket.

It was safe there, though and I stayed there often. Flat-sitting with pleasure, looking after her cats when she was away. Andy ran a good house. She'd studied and now constantly practised interior design, constantly rebuilding or decorating some part, nook or crevice of her house. She never sat still and the space benefited from her. She kept cats for company but her biggest pet love was pigs: mugs, tea towels, banks, cuddly things, they got their snout into everything and turned the kitchen pink. Of course it meant that nobody ever had an excuse for not getting her a present she liked. She made life easier for everyone. It was the one thing that brought Andy down from being my big sister to being my sister. She was sussed, got her life together – with all the usual boy problems a voracious blonde twenty-five-year-old encounters; and was capable of acting with responsibility like a grown-up. The little piggy thing was the area in which Andy allowed the child in her to be indulged. Providing a companion that fell between two very apparent worlds.

I could talk to Andy. I'd been doing a lot of that the past few weeks. Feeling my bosses' eyes bearing into the back of my neck in the open-plan office where I worked if I was doing too much talking and not enough typing. Mostly, the subject matter was Jenks. I loved him dearly, trusted nobody more, but his words were twisting with my brain, my logic, my reason. It worked on many different levels, all psychological, all mind-fucks, but the one argument that always seemed to precede Jenks hastily throwing razors and clothes into his sports bag, threatening to walk out, usually started with a discussion on 'whether I was really naive or extremely calculating.' I didn't understand what he meant by 'calculating.' I also didn't understand anything about coming down. Basically it's the opposite of being high and as acute as the highs are obtuse.

In these angry times I cried and pogoed around the green living room to a lot of New Order or sang their songs while kicking the bins that lined the roads of Crystal Palace where we lived, looking for release in their fatalistic souredness. In the end it was me who walked out. Me, Kat! I never thought I'd do that. Nine days before, on Halloween. After a glass full of frustration and frozen vodka smashed into another dimension on the wall behind me. I said nothing. I just left the room. Then left his life to save mine. I needed sanity.

THE ONLY thing Andy enjoyed doing more than throwing parties was going to parties. And this was *the* party. Nothing was going to stop me being there – even the end of my summer with Jenks. This was the end of several chapters at once. We arrived at The Park in Kensington far earlier than usual that night. The only thing that mattered was making sure we got in – everything else was assured after that. And seeing as half of London would want to be in there, the earlier we got there the better.

There never seemed to be any waiting around at Shoom, however early you arrived – it always seemed to be the height of the party. Only some of the highs were higher than others. Velvet limbs. Dewdrop heads. Lush physicality everywhere. Andy and I stood up on the balcony watching it all go on. The lights bouncing off the white shroud that canopied the dancefloor and back up to us, reflected in smiley eyes. It felt good. It felt better. It felt like the way you were meant to feel – could feel – all the time, and that we would just after tasting it once. Forever.

Ronnie found us there. We were pleased to see Ronnie. We were always pleased to see Ronnie. He'd saved us something special. Little pink pills. From Amsterdam. He made an art of his job. He looked after us. Made sure we didn't get any snide gear. A fake. Soon we'd merged with the heat. The intensity. Became part of it all. Shoom had its own atmosphere, like any other separately orbiting planet. Opaque, misty and warm like a birthing pool. The condensation rising from the dancers' glowing bodies melted with the dry ice, making the climate thick and cloudy. Comforting, reassuring, a mist of resuscitated souls. Arms breaking free – touching the stars. Jon's pink wrist watch waving above the clouds . . . Perfect. Everybody is there. Jenks too. We kiss for the last time. Lights up. Last record. Last time. No more encores. No more: 'one more!' It feels right to complete the cycle. At the end of the night we repeat the ritual one last time; into a cab and off to Kensal Rise. As he held the door of the black cab open for me and I climbed in through the crook of his arm I ripped the seat of my black velvet trousers from left cheek to centre. They were my favourite party trousers. I felt their loss. Even they weren't entering the next stage with me. My bright white, long-sleeved 'Pure' T-shirt just covering the whiteness of my bottom as I tucked it under me and sat down on the pull-down seat.

USUALLY IF we'd stayed over at the weekend, Saturday would begin very leisurely with the horse racing or Sunday with *The Waltons*. You were still always a bit too excited to sleep for long after a night like that. Then we'd all go down the pub for a drink. Ross always said you'd wasted your E money if you didn't drink the day after. But I enjoyed the freshly-hoovered feeling of my morning-after brain too much to want to cloak it in alcohol. We spent hours in that pub with its sawdust covered floors.

Today was different. This late morning awakening was more reflective. Solitary. Jenks gone. Our last night together. Reconciled for this night. Proof that we'd be friends. Just time. That's all we needed. Jude had gone to work; poor thing. Ross, down at Sainsbury's in Ladbroke Grove, getting the shopping in. It was all different. But I was quite happy. Things change. We have to go with the flow. Our lives unfold. Transition time, once again. I was content. Just lying. Thinking. Drinking tea. I tied the foldaway bed up into its sofa-self for the last time. And went to get a shower. Looking forward to my day off. Wondering what I would do with the time. Looking forward to the feeling of water jets massaging my body. Looking after me. Refreshment. Renewal. The club-stickiness of my hair rinsed out. No more scent of cigarette smoke. Clean.

The front door clicked. Ross was home. 'I brought you a towel.' I hadn't even realised there wasn't one.

'Thanks,' I cried through the steam hoping my voice would be heard wherever he was in the flat by now. Probably putting away the groceries. I felt a draught. The shower curtain had been drawn back. By Ross. Naked Ross. Stepping in . . . I didn't want this. The shampoo got in my eyes. It was supposed to be mild but it stung. I couldn't get out of the way. Squashed into the corner, pressed into the tiles, I felt I couldn't breathe. I felt faint. I felt small. I felt numb.

His pressure gone, I slumped. Collapsed on the edge of the shower. The bathroom felt clammy. The creeping, distasteful chill of cold, scared sweat filling the space between the shower and the brown folded towel he'd brought that lay at the foot of the door.

I said nothing. I left. I went back to Andy's. She wasn't there. I sat on the stairs and waited for her to call. She didn't. I thought of my other girlfriend. Ruby. Ten years older than me. Like consulting the oracle. Like mother and daughter. I stalled. I dialled the number. I told her what happened. I let go. I cried. She said I didn't stand a chance. That nobody would believe it. And people would be hurt. And there could be no point going to the police. Brutal truths. I felt trapped. I felt alone. I felt guilty. I contacted the Family Planning Association. If it was an emergency, I could see someone in Brick Lane. They couldn't see me until tomorrow morning. I didn't know what to do. I washed. I went into work. I gathered up a crew and went down the pub. Sat in the corner playing word-association games that seemed to predominantly feature the Blackpool Tower. Drank tequila. Got blasted. And felt for the first time that I didn't want to feel what was real. Made it go away.

At the family planning clinic – the claustrophobic female doctor tried to persuade me to go on the Pill to prevent any further 'accidents.' There was no love between us women. No camaraderie. No support. Empty-handed, she made me take the little pills in front of her to make sure – ridiculously – they were for me, that I wasn't getting them for someone else. Fat chance, I thought. Here, downtown Detroit. Anywhere.

Emily Perkins

'THE INDELIBLE HULK'

'Hello?'

'Maxine? It's me. Bloody hell. I have had the most horrible day. Do you know what Peter said to me? That I was slacking around. And I wasn't. Do you know why I think he's such a shit? Because he fancies me. Not being vain or anything, but. He does. It's obvious to anyone. Do you know what he does? He avoids me on purpose. Can you believe that! As if we were at school or something and he was going to put a spider on my chair—'

This is Etta. She's a friend of Maxine's (more on that in a sec). To give you a proper idea of how she sounds, try imagining the above with every second word italicized: *I* have had *the* most *horrible* day, Do you *know* what he *said* . . . etcetera. The lack of niceties to begin the conversation, the straightforward launch into personal detail, is typical. Also the ingenious technique of posing the question herself and immediately vocalising an answer, thus saving Maxine the need to speak or even think. So far, so considerate. Then, once the story has reached a conclusion – Etta is a brave and courageous story-teller, unafraid of anti-climax or lack of content – she will pause for breath. Maxine knows what's coming.

'So. *Anyway*. *How* are *you*?'

You'd think she was asking whether or not Maxine's cancer is in remission, not that Maxine has cancer, but such is the tone of deep concern dripping from each syllable. But the tone isn't the really astonishing thing, condescending as it is. No, what really gets Maxine groping for her cigarette lighter is that *as Etta asks*

141

the question, i.e. immediately she's stopped jawing on about herself, Maxine can hear her fingers start to rattle over the computer keyboard. The unmistakable flicker of fingers that have taken a three-week intensive touch typing course clattering surely over the keys: Dear Bill So good to see you yesterday I'm thrilled with your thoughts on the Such and Such merger – And so Maxine's face falls a little and she says Fine Etta, I'm fine thanks a lot, yep, everything's going OK here, really, really fine.

The obvious question is, what's Maxine doing with someone like Etta for her Best Friend? (sorry about the use of *best friend*: grown women using these two words are just asking to be visualized in rompers and pigtails, holding hands in a circle having shunted some unfortunate child out of it, chanting Na na na-nah na in sing-song unison – but that's the way Maxine insists on describing Etta). The worst thing is this description only goes one way. Etta is almost Maxine's *only* friend, while Etta has three or four Bestest Friends she'd rate over Maxine any day of the week. It's not that she's genuinely close to these women, it's that she believes them to be cooler and therefore more desirable than Maxine. She'll blow Maxine out for an invitation from Mee-Mee at ten minutes' notice. So why does Maxine put up with all this? For the answer, we have to quickly rewind thirteen years.

Maxine is fourteen years old. Her height is five feet and two inches and she weighs fourteen stone. That's fourteen times fourteen pounds. Her younger brother, the maths genius, can tell her that that is one hundred and ninety-six pounds, nearly point oh four of a pound for every day she's been alive counting Leap days, and if she continues at this rate she'll weigh seven hundred and ninety-three pounds, or fifty-six and a half stone, by

the time she's seventy, assuming she stays alive that l̖
Maxine says nothing. Her mother, who at thirty-six yeȧ
old only ever weighs a clean one hundred and ten pounds,
looks at her and says, 'It's not your glands, honey, and it's not
your genes. I just don't know.' Still Maxine says nothing. Al, her
mother's boyfriend, punches her dimpled shoulder and says,
'You can join the circus, Max, and keep us in our old age.'
Maxine goes to her room and quietly closes the door.

Maxine's brother the maths genius is one rung above her on
the school social ladder. This is not saying a lot, as Maxine
belongs to the small core of outcast children. These are not your
regular social rejects. Those kids are the science nerds and the
late developers and the Dungeons and Dragons obsessives, and
Maxine's brother is all three of these at once. While they're
never invited to parties, they are pitied rather than derided, and
at least stick together in a sweaty little band of geekness. They
hold their own parties, where there are Rubik's Cube speed
competitions and no girls. The outcasts never have parties. The
outcasts don't associate with each other. Only one thing would
be worse than being an outcast, and that would be acknowl-
edging it by befriending another one. The outcasts maintain the
illusion that they are loners, solo by choice, and they are more
acutely aware of the social pegging within the school than ninety-
five per cent of the other students.

The most recognizable outcasts are: Maxine because of the
sheer bulk of her; a girl with a stutter who shaved off her
eyebrows on a dare and whose outcast status was confirmed
when they never grew back; another fat kid, a boy who has the
unfortunate extra distinction of smelling like human shit; and a
skinny older boy who flies into the most extraordinary spiralling
rages every month or so, after which he'll sit and blub so hard

that snot comes out his nose. The other kids treat him with some respect although he is an outcast, mainly because he can fling chairs and smash his fist through doors and rumour has it that he bears a grudge.

Now at this point I'd like to offer you a little reassurance: Maxine is not fat any more. Chances are you'd disapprove of an obese heroine, no matter how many other qualities she possessed. Fatness in adults, you'll secretly agree, is an indicator of weakness, self-indulgence, and torpor. Indulgence, torpor – mouth the words, they even *sound* rotund, plump, chubby. Don't give me that rubbish about glands and metabolisms. Lardy people have slow metabolisms because they're fat, right? Not the other way round! Ever seen a fat person eating? It's a simple truth – they eat more. And lazy, they're so *lazy*, fat people, they like nothing better than to roll around on the sofa all day long jamming lemon buns into their well-covered throats.

Anyway anyway, that's enough. I think I'm letting a note of personal disgust creep in. It won't happen again. All you need to know is, after years of struggle, Maxine's a normal 'overweight' girl, a 'big' girl, not an out-and-out fatty. But let's head back to the days when she was.

Auditions for the school play. A familiar scenario. Cute, confident kids encouraged by their pushy parents, belting out '*It's a beautiful day – tomorrow*' at the tops of their lungs; the music teacher with her wrap-around skirt and faint smell of sweat smiling, tapping time with her baton; the ginger kid who surprises everyone by pulling out a fantastic tap-dance routine; and the gorgeous, soulful youth reciting *Desiderata* and giving all the girls (and some of the boys) the 'absolute chills'. Maxine is not a part of this montage. Maxine is inside a cubicle in the girls' bathroom waiting till she's sure no one is there before she comes out. She'd do this on an ordinary day, just because it's easier to deal with being alone in an empty room than being alone in a room full of chattering, mirror-examining girls. But today she's got a special reason for waiting.

Maxine is wearing a men's XL T-shirt she has borrowed from her mother's boyfriend. It is black with metallic grey lettering, in fake handwriting, that says *Sticks and stones may break my bones but whips and chains excite me.* It also has a cartoon picture of a bobbly-eyed male figure on all fours wearing a dog collar. Al was given it by his pals at the model-making club, as a joke. The soft rolls of Maxine's breasts and stomach are visible through the fabric. On her bottom half is a pair of turquoise Lycra leggings, strained at the seams. Her feet are spilling over from stacked orange sandals with fabric thongs. In her hand is a plastic bag full of cosmetics she has nicked from her mother's dressing table. As soon as she hears total silence outside the cubicle she opens the door and lurches forward on her sandals to make up her face.

There's a reason Maxine's putting herself through the potential humiliation of auditioning. She knows the lead part will almost definitely be awarded to Lucia Brabazon, the tall dark rich girl who is admired by everyone and yet manages somehow to stay slightly aloof from every clique. More than anything in the world, Maxine wants to be Lucia Brabazon's friend. If the other kids saw her walking down the hall with Lucia Brabazon, if they were noticed eating lunch together, if a rumour even went round that Maxine had been to Lucia Brabazon's house, her social troubles would be over. This is why Maxine is going all out to impress the auditioning panel and

145

to secure the third-to-main part, of the heroine's best friend, in the school play.

The ladies and gentlemen of the panel are: First, Mr Gibbon, the HoD for English. When you meet Mr Gibbon the first thing you wonder is if he was born looking like his name, or if he grew into it. Second, Ms Schmidt, the Head Woman, who is on the panel because her job is so completely token it's just about non-existent and she never has anything to do on Thursday afternoons anyway. And the glamour factor is represented by Mr Anthony ('call me Tone') McCavity, the guest director, an old boy of the school who now appears sporadically in the local newspaper publicizing one of his avant-garde theatrical extravaganzas. The school play has in fact been devised especially by Tone, and concerns his exploits as a naive youth and the passionate student romance he enjoyed with a girl who, he now says to himself, looked remarkably like that gorgeous long-legged brunette girl standing by the fire exit. Yes, he thinks, she'll be his Juliet, she'll definitely raise the Tone, and he snorts inwardly at his hilarious pun. She must be all of sixteen. He's determined to get a hand between those legs before the rehearsal period's over.

So these are the fine minds that will be judging our Maxine's performance and deciding whether or not she goes through to phase two of the auditions – a personal interview with Tone McCavity to see if the student is on the right 'wavelength'. Meanwhile, Maxine is emerging from the toilets, white as a sheet. Nerves? No, her mother's super-blanched concealer stick, applied in great sweeping smudges over her suety face. Within this, black Gothic kohl covering an area around each eye the size of what her grandfather would call 'a shiner'. And smeared over the mouth, pale coral lips. The effect is a hybrid of a Kabuki mask and a sticky lollipop that's been left sweating in the sun. Her pallid hair has been given a bit of a lift with some glitter gel, spiking it up into meringue-like crusts. She looks like nothing her school has ever seen. She looks terrific.

The panel sit on their bench seat, notepads on their laps, heads drooping slightly after the third under-developed boy has sung 'Inchworm' from Hans Christian Andersen, with extra pathos on account of his tiny size. Tone McCavity is edging away from Ms Schmidt who has just sighed, tossed her hair and crossed her legs so that her skirt's ridden up, giving him an eyeful of tanned, mature knee. The music teacher is consulting with the pianist as to who's next and which piece of music is needed. She's cursing herself again for leaving the music to *Godspell* at home. A lot of the popular girls are unhappy that they have to sing the pebble song unaccompanied. Lucia Brabazon has been announcing in a loud voice that it's *far* less professional than the open call for *The Dream* at the Town Hall last month and several girls have been nodding and muttering, Yes, just what sort of 'call' is this, sending resentment back through the queue of students in angry ripples.

Maxine wants to have her go now. She can see that Lucia's getting restless and is worried that she might leave in a huff. While the music teacher is flicking through the sheets of music with the pianist, Maxine lumbers up the stairs and waddles forward to centre stage.

Tone McCavity hears a giggle and looks up from Ms Schmidt's exposed knee and, fuck me, thigh. 'Oh my god,' he says, out loud. 'Who? Is that?'

Mrs Schmidt fumbles with her glasses, which she's been rubbing across her collarbone in a reverie. She peers. 'Oh. That's Maxine'.

Tone McCavity makes a ticking noise with his tongue. 'This is not a freak show. This is a serious drama.'

There's a throat-clearing rumble from Gibbon. 'All the students must have a fair chance', he says.

'Well sure', says Tone. 'If you think it's *fair* to let her stand up there one minute longer.'

As he says this, it does look as if Maxine's lost her nerve. She glances over to the side of the stage and starts moving her body in that direction. But she's only handing a cassette to the speccy kid with the ghetto blaster. Back in the middle of the rostrum, she nods at him. The spring's number one song starts – Olivia Newton-John singing 'Let's get physical, physical, I wanna get physicah-ah-al let's get into physical.' And Maxine's larger than average body starts to talk.

Luckily for Maxine, she's concentrating too hard on the music to hear the hall erupting in laughter. Unluckily, they're still howling when the tape finishes and she leans forward, bending as much as she can in the middle, to take her bow. And as the general hilarity dies down she hears one of the cruellest sounds in the world: the sound of an unsuccessfully restrained snigger. She turns her head towards it. Leaning against the red velvet curtain, looking impossibly poised for her age, is leggy Lucia Brabazon. Her hand is covering her luscious mouth and she's shaking with laughter as one of the boys who's not auditioning but came to skip class anyway says to her – 'Jesus Christ did you see the fat lesbian? More like the Incredible Hulk.' Lucia Brabazon doesn't even stop laughing when Maxine looks her dead in the eye.

Now, if Maxine was a different type of person, if she was, in the current jargon, 'a survivor', she'd have turned this situation to her advantage. You'd see her on chat shows plugging her latest stand-up tour and she'd say, 'Well it was all an accident how I got into comedy really, I wanted to be a serious performer but at my first audition I made everybody laugh, so. Here I am.' And, if asked for details, she might shift in her comfy television chair and say, 'Well I was a fat girl you see,' and the interviewer would say, 'No never,' thinking, I bloody bet you were as well, you're still on the hefty side, and Maxine'd say, 'Oh yes I was, really I had a weight problem, I had a troubled relationship with food and the other kids all laughed at me.' And the audience would go 'Ah' because they'd been touched by someone who was usually so jolly and funny, but look she's just like all us ordinary folk really. And Maxine would know they were pitying her and think, Fuck you Lucia Brabazon, I hope you're watching because I make more money in one appearance than you could if you took your clothes off for a month.

But, as we've probably established, Maxine is not that kind of girl. She is not a two-fingers, proud to be different, defiant chick. All she wants is to be normal. So when she hears the snorting – when she sees Lucia snicker and buckle at the knee as the boy leans closer – she doesn't tough it out and make like the routine was intentionally funny. Confusion shows on her face. She's panting from the exertion and she needs a glass of water. She doesn't know how to move, how to get off the stage. She's stuck. And so she stands there, a cringing grin plastered on her face, breathing hard and wondering how the hell she's going to get home.

That was then. This is now and, like I said, there have been some improvements. She's keeping the weight down, she's got a flattering haircut, she's learned about crucial things like dark block colours and vertical stripes. Three years ago she took part in an assertiveness training course and acquired some useful positive affirmations for the really low moments. But there's still the small problem of trustworthy friends. She doesn't have any. Life outside of school isn't really that different. The social structures seem to be pretty much the same, and though she's tried hard to re-invent herself Maxine still wakes each morning feeling the brand of Outcast on her forehead, though she shakes her head as if to remove it and smiles at herself in the mirror, saying *You're the greatest*. Also she retains her ability to spot another outcast at fifty paces, and cross to the other side of the room. It's likely that Etta only befriended her so she could have the requisite fat friend to stand next to at drinks parties, making her own figure appear even more sylph-like.

Lately though, Maxine hasn't seen much of Etta. There's not a lot of her to see, boom boom. But really, Etta's cancelled the last three arrangements they've made to meet up. Three. And all at the last minute. Maxine isn't sure if Etta's trying to drop her as a friend or if she's just being phenomenally rude. She even let a note of annoyance creep into her voice last time she was accepting Etta's lame excuses and Etta got very defensive. No need to be like *that*, I think she said. No need to get *snippy*, Maxine. Don't have a *hissy* fit. So Maxine had backed down, apologized herself, said, Of course she understood, don't worry, that's fine, how about Etta comes round for videos next Thursday night?

So, it's Thursday.

'Maxine? It's me.'

Oh dear.

'Hi Etta. Are you still on for tonight?' Maxine's been thinking about popcorn and Häagen-Dazs all day.

'Ah. Well. This is the thing. Could we make it another night?'

'Oh. Are you busy?'

'Mm, it's bloody *work*. I'm going to *have* to stay late.'

'Well come round late, it's no problem. It's only Friday tomorrow.'

'Oh, *thanks*, but. Mn. I really can't. I *could* be here for *ages*.'

'Oh. OK. Well, how about next week then?'

'Yeahmaybe. That'd be *great*. Uh, I'll call you.'

Maxine hangs up quietly. She gets the videos anyway and makes microwave nachos to eat in front of them. At eight o'clock she tries Etta's direct line at the office, to see if she's anywhere near finishing. The voice-mail picks up. She tries again at half past. Still no answer. Maybe she's on her way over. At nine-thirty Maxine dials the number for Etta's house, just to see how she is. It rings and rings. Etta must've forgotten to switch her machine on. Maxine stares into space, her mouth open, just drifting, then jolts out of it when the ringing abruptly stops.

'Hello?' someone's shouting.

'Hello?' says Maxine.

She can hear the whirr and clatter of conversation, music, a clunking sound like bits of crockery being banged together.

'Ahgin bunder wha?' shouts the man at Etta's house.

'What?' shouts Maxine. 'I can't understand you?'

'Etta!' Maxine feels the rush of the phone receiver being held out into Etta's living room, with a sweeping moving noise. 'Etta!' the guy yells again. Then Maxine can hear a fuzzy, close exchange.

'Who is it?' This is Etta's voice, mumbling, to the man.

'Some woman.'

'What did she say?'

'Don't know.'

'Did she – oh . . .' Maxine can hear Etta sigh. 'Look I can't take it.'

151

'What'll I say?'

'I don't know. Oh just hang up. Hang *up*.'

And Maxine feels herself being clunked down hard on the floor. She gives the walls and ceiling her bewildered look and puts her fingers to her mouth. Oh, she says. Oh. She exhales, but not too much, and turns back towards the video screen. Everything's blurry and wet. She blinks at it a few times until it's clear again. Pats the sofa for the remote contol and presses play.

The next morning, Maxine wakes up with a smile. She heaves herself out of bed and stands in front of the head-to-shoulders mirror above her chest of drawers. You're the greatest, she says, as she has every morning since she completed the assertiveness training. You're the greatest, she repeats, and dimples at her reflection. She won't be seeing Etta again, she realizes with something close to relief. Nothing's really changed. She's got one less friend, that's all, taking her total to zero. Well, there are the girls at work, and there's her mother and her mother's new boyfriend, the neighbours: there is some human contact. The picture's not that bleak, she says out loud, and smiles again. She remembers being fourteen and the promise she'd made to herself after walking off that stage, to one day find a true friend. You will, she says to the mirror. You're the greatest.

And this, I think, is Maxine's triumph. It's not much of one, as triumphs go, but it's real. Maxine's small victory is over Etta, and it's over Lucia Brabazon as well. In spite of everything she knows, she doesn't give up an idea of friendship that one day she'll achieve. She piles her bowl high with cereal and pours over lo-fat milk. Maybe this evening she'll go to a movie. She washes and dries her bowl and spoon, puts them away in the cupboard. Cleans her teeth. Hums a little tune to herself, in her high, sweet voice.

Jenny Ross

'THE IMMORTALS'

'I spy with my little eye something beginning with *A*,' Bill offered with more enthusiasm than I could ever muster up.

'Inside or outside?'

'Outside . . .'

'Asteroid?'

'Your turn.'

Two-and-a-half years in space and where does it get you? Playing the most tedious game of I Spy since the only words you knew were car and doggie.

'Your turn,' Bill insisted.

I noticed something on the edge of my vision. 'I spy with my little eye something beginning with *S,C,C*.'

'Would that be . . . suspended cryogenic chambers?' Bill strained to bring the two floating, silver coffins into view. Rental time's up my little frozen friends; time to take you back to Mummy Earth.

Just as we were getting over our long overdue discovery there was an enormous crack of thunder, stars flicked off in the sky like a bar at closing time. Our craft lurched right, left and then flipped straight over. My heart fell into the pit of my stomach, hovered around my lower kidneys and finally settled for a resting place just to the right of my neo-cortex. My skull was throbbing like a kinky politician's pants in a Soho club. Wisps of light flashed by like streakers at a football match and then there was silence, stillness and a warm feeling in my

155

knickers that brought with it the distinct scent of childhood humiliation.

'Harry? Harriet? You okay?' Bill was standing over me. He had a four-inch gash just beneath his right temple.

I straightened myself, attempting to regain my composure. 'Check our co-ordinates, we shouldn't be this near the sun.'

'Harriet, that's not the sun . . .' Bill looked awkward, nervous, upset.

'Uranus is on fire?'

'A bit closer to home.'

There'd been many times in my life I had thought, how on Earth did I get myself into a fix like this? But now with Earth gone and us the only survivors left, I felt it was an appropriate – albeit rather tactless – thought to have as I opened the First Aid kit to plaster Bill's bleeding head.

As I administered the bandage I pondered how inside the human brain there are three basic responses to ensure our survival. The first is to run or hide – we had nowhere to run to and nowhere to hide. The second was to fight – we had no one to fight, which left the third option for survival, that old chestnut, procreation. The fun option. Me and Bill exchanged smouldering looks before we realized with only two humans left in existence and only one genetic line, by the third generation down our children would begin to look like members of royalty and that could be drastic. We needed to create two genetic lines or accept that the children of the future would be hideously deformed. Sure, we didn't have anywhere to bring them up as of yet but we'd worry about that later.

As we stood over the two thawing cryogenic chambers I became an internal cocktail of three parts sorrow, two parts fear and one part something I couldn't quite put my finger on . . . well, at least not in public, anyway.

'You know I heard a rumour that the woman in Chamber 90210 used to be a porn star.' Bill's eyes lit up at his statement. It was the first time I'd seen him raise a smile in days, at least I hoped that's all he was raising.

'Where did you read that, the *International Enquirer*?' I condescended.

'U-huh. She had a really distinctive name . . . Lilith, that was it. Lilith L'Amour. Rumour has it she was having an affair with the President when his wife found out and put out a hit on her. He was so in love with Lilith he had her injected out into space to ensure her safety.' It was the stupidest story I had ever heard, apart from the one I found myself presently acting out. I hadn't the foggiest about either of these human hams on ice, but the one in the other chamber had a message engraved on the front of his capsule: 'Greetings alien friends! My name is Brad Hammer, I come in peace.' Boy, was Brad in for a big disappointment.

Lilith sat with a thermal blanket wrapped round her Amazon shoulders, sipping freeze-dried coffee. Over half a century asleep and she wakes up with all her make-up intact, not a hair out of place, like a scene from some daytime space opera. She pulled herself to her feet and peered out of the oval starhole.

'Gee, two suns, where are we? I thought it was kind of hot around here,' she squeaked.

I thought now was as good a time as any to break the news to her that the second sun was in fact the burning remains of our home planet. I expected her to be upset but instead she commented that if she went up onto the flight deck she'd get an even tan without having to turn every 30 minutes.

Statements like that eroded my sense of hope about the future of the human race. Here we were, alone in the galaxy, and all she could do was think of ways to promote skin cancer.

I glanced over at Bill. He still hadn't broken the news to Brad but you couldn't blame him. Brad had been howling like an abandoned baby ever since Bill told him *Star Trek: The Next Generation* had been cancelled halfway through the Generation After Next.

'Why? Why? Why?' Brad spluttered into his James T Kirk mug. I could see Bill struggling to put it diplomatically and decided to intervene.

'It was a very popular show, it ran until the end of . . . er . . . well the end of . . . um . . . life as we know it?'

'Are you trying to humour me?'

'Er . . . no.' Breaking bad news was like pulling off plasters – best to make it quick and painless. I switched my tone, becoming a mother comforting a small child. 'I'm sorry to have to tell you this, Brad, but . . . Earth just blew up and we're the last four humans in the stratosphere.' At first he looked confused, giving it time to sink in. Then a broad grin broke out across his swollen face and his dark eyes, that I'd at first likened to two piss-holes in the snow, began to brighten.

'Does this mean I actually get to *be* Captain Jean-Luc Picard?'

'Can I be Lieutenant Uhura?' Lilith piped up from behind him. Bill and I looked towards each other, disdain barely veiled by our sense of inner panic. We put them under sedation whilst we decided what to do. The future of mankind was in our hands and this was no time for role-play.

Bill and I crept down to the chill-out bay to listen to some transcendental river music. It was calming but I had a weak bladder and the trickle percussion became annoying after the first three tracks. We switched for the lounge/jungle fusion of *The Best of The Carpenters* which was quite mellow until 'Calling Occupants Of Interplanetary Craft' came on and reminded us we had work to do. Up on deck, we stood staring at our two new companions. We knew it was rude but we couldn't help ourselves, mesmerized by the rhythmic rise and fall of Lilith's breasts. It was kind of peaceful until Brad started snoring like an asthmatic in charge of a smoke machine.

Brad woke in a sulk and Lilith didn't look much happier. I tried to coax them out of their moods with the offer of a game of I Spy but they weren't impressed. I cut to brass tacks and figured if we had to mate with these people, we might as well start where the rest of the human race used to – a polite bit of small talk. 'So Brad,' I offered him a reassuring grin, 'what brought you to outer space?'

He explained to us how he had funded his journey into the future with his earnings from the Lottery. The guy had won it three times in a row! After two years of chicks, Ferraris, more chicks, Porsches, cruises and more cocaine than a post-Oscars party he had a revelation. 'I lost interest in Armani, Gucci and Dolce & Gabbana and began to find myself strangely attracted to open-toed sandals. It was then that I realized I was the Son of God.'

It was then that we realized it wasn't the thermal pressure that was affecting his brain as we had first thought. Granted the man had been frozen for sixty years. Who wouldn't go a bit crazy after turning on the defrost, only to realize your toenails have grown in spirals back around your own foot and your home planet is doing a hauntingly convincing impression of an over-cooked meatball? But Lilith had been through the cryogenic mill as well and in spite of being the most puerile person I'd ever met, she appeared relatively sane, if not a bit space sick. Bill seemed to like her, hardly surprising when you consider she had breasts that could crack walnuts. By the second day, Brad's egocentric behaviour had reached fever pitch and we were all in agreement he was as cuckoo as a Swiss clock maker. Well we would have been, except Lilith didn't get it!

We locked Brad in the hold in the belly of the craft. Occasionally we'd let Lilith go down and watch him since it reminded her of the low budget shows on cable. By the fourth day, he'd begun to live on a diet of his own sperm. He looked relatively healthy. After all, it does have two meals' worth of protein in it – or so some smug bloke told me once – but by the expression on Brad's face I felt pretty fortunate I wasn't the one having to take heed of this information. As I watched him tuck in for seconds, I reasoned it probably only worked if it was someone else's sperm you were eating. Still . . . nothing ventured, nothing gained.

I felt sorry for the guy but that's what you get for going around somebody else's spaceship acting like Christopher Columbus on his last voyage back from Mexico. I pressed the intercom and immediately he was into his mad-dog routine. He was even foaming at the mouth. Must've been hungry earlier. 'You'll never take my sperm! If this be the seed of life, let my belly be full!' Look at him go! He was like a squirrel who'd forgotten to gather any nuts until he noticed some snow on the ground. He mumbled something vague about penis envy and then got back to the task in hand.

'You see, with quantum theory dynamics, the Earth's demise is part of the universal shift that will create other lives in far-off galaxies. For every reaction there is an equal and opposite reaction. Yin and Yang — the energy that Earth's explosion generated is all part of the atomic reaction that created the galaxy when the Big Bang first occurred.' Bill was gesticulating so wildly I feared he might take flight. From the look on Lilith's face, I could tell he was no nearer to communicating the theory to her, but he seemed to be enjoying himself and it kept them occupied. 'The universe is expanding outwards and will eventually implode in on itself.'

'Are you telling me I'm going to implode in on myself anyway? I knew I should've got those silicon implants.' She let out a laugh befitting a neutered horse. Maybe it was the way her nostrils flared as she did it, or maybe it was the way it whinnied numbly off the microflec surface of the ship, but it was definitely an equestrian experience. 'Say, do you think you could tell me how that space-loo works again?'

As Bill began to explain to her how to flush a space toilet for the third time, I realized he wasn't so much trying to enlighten her on the subject of universal forces as trying to get a better view down her abundance of cleavage. They were getting a bit too close for comfort and there was no way I'd be procreating with Brad. I cut my losses and offered to take her to the toilet myself.

'You women, still going to the toilets in pairs,' Bill looked disappointed.

As the lift doors closed I tactically countered, 'I may as well get over the little chat we'll need to have about space menstruation.' It was the perfect decoy. I could even see him cringing as the doors slid shut.

'You know, I can't remember the last time I had my period.' Lilith sucked on a lacquered nail. So that was why she kept vomiting; I'd thought it was hibernation sickness. It was probably just as well she was already pregnant, at the rate Brad was eating his own sperm. I left her puking in the toilet and promised to return and flush.

Down on the cargo decks, the cryogenic space coffins Brad and Lilith had dreamed would project them into the world of the future lay empty, the odd bit of dry ice still making its bid for fresh carbon.

Lilith teetered into view, a vision in green embroiled in a luminous pink twin-set. I'd have to get her out of it and her breasts seemed to be agreeing with me, straining at the taut fabric. I had a spare space-suit in my closet. It would be a bit baggy around some areas but at least it would be better than launching her into the future wearing something both the gender and fashion police would lock her away for without a key. She rummaged through her personal belongings. Humming quietly to herself, she took out her compact, powdered her nose and applied lipstick complaining that it had started to smell a bit since thawing. 'What does it matter anyway?' I queried

'Don't you think Bill's kind of cute?' Lilith licked her lips. To be honest, it had never really crossed my mind, but now she mentioned it I guess he had avoided being beaten with a stick marked ugly. Having sex with him wouldn't be that gross as long as I got to him before she did. There was a reason I'd never slept with anyone in high school and I wasn't about to start taking sloppy seconds now. 'Such a good lover as well.'

I held that thought.

As I lay in my cabin listening to the sounds of banging which I'd assumed was Brad trying to escape the night before, I wondered to myself how I could have slept through that frantic owl noise Lilith was now making. I could barely remember the last time I'd had sex, but listening to them in the next cabin made me feel kind of lonely and a little bit horny. I was the captain of this craft! If anyone was going to go around having sex, it should be me, for God's sake! Lilith was already pregnant. What Bill was doing was beyond the call of duty. Still, I wondered, when did duty ever have anything to do with basic urges?

I wandered down to the cargo deck and selected another one of the videos Brad had brought along. I was getting quite into *The X-Files*, the only thing that disturbed me about them was the way the crazy guys were always so sincere. Maybe Brad really was the Son of God. Maybe it'd been God who had rigged the Lottery. Maybe the truth wasn't out there, but in here gorging himself on his own sperm . . . maybe I'd watched too much television.

I crept down to the hold to watch him, in need of an ally. He sat in the corner, an amazed expression carved upon his ashen face. He seemed calm enough. In truth he appeared to be in a kind of catatonic state. I took a chance and entered. He was barely breathing but as I reached out to take his pulse he spoke: 'Harriet, I think I'm pregnant.'

As we stood over Brad, watching the monitor, I was filled with a sense of hope. Somehow, against all odds, facing the demise of our race, this man had managed to procreate with himself. I had read of such things happening in rare breeds of tropical toads. It was logically possible that Brad could have done the same, after all, he was not unlike a toad. Either that or it was the Second Coming. Or in Brad's case, the hundred and sixty-second. Lilith didn't look convinced by any of my explanations. Either that or she was trying to understand them. She played with her necklace, 'Have any of you ever seen that film *Alien?*'

What had we been thinking of, defrosting these people in the first place? They had so many conspiracy theories, they made Oliver Stone look like a novice. I made her stand outside for a second whilst I suggested to Bill that we cut our losses and stick them back into space. He wasn't too keen on that idea; apparently he'd fallen in love with Lilith and couldn't bear to be separated from her now that he'd found her. To be honest, I couldn't bear another night listening to the echoes of their frenzied lovemaking. This spaceship wasn't big enough for the four of us. Someone had to go. I let Lilith back into the room.

'That guy in the film had an alien in his stomach. It came out and killed the whole crew. I say we kill him.' She grabbed hold of Bill's hand, squeezing authoritatively.

'I say we kill him too,' Bill echoed pathetically. What was he, a Stepford Husband? The spineless traitor. I wasn't going to have this B-movie extra giving me orders on my own god-damned ship.

'If it is an alien baby in his stomach, surely they're going to come back and get it if they went to the bother of impregnating him in the first place,' I fumed. 'All we've got to do is sit it out without killing each other until they get here.'

'They'll kill us all,' she insisted, pulling at her hair for effect.

'We don't need an alien race to come and annihilate us, we've already done that ourselves. Now you either shut up or get back into that human refrigerator where you belong.'

Lilith looked towards Bill for support.

'What does it matter anyway? We're just sitting around waiting to implode,' he shrugged, bringing the argument to a close.

* * *

'The Immortals'

As I stood with the father-to-be, waving good-bye to the two cryogenic chambers heading out into space with a 'Just Refrigerated' sign on the back and some empty fuel cans we'd added just to get into the spirit of the occasion, I thought it was probably for the best that we had decided to go our separate ways. Humans, eh? Can't live with them, can't live without them. We'd be back for them when we'd found somewhere to set up base. *If* we found somewhere.

I gazed across at Brad nursing his swollen stomach. He may be a bit crazy, but he was pregnant his hormones were all over the place. We may be the last of the traditional humans but that might not be a bad thing, I reasoned. Bill and Lilith were in a worse position: living ice-pops in some remote space museum to the human race that would be open to infinity and beyond.

Brad and I didn't know how far the ship would take us. We didn't know if we'd ever find other life forms. We didn't even know if Brad was going to give birth to one, but we went in the spirit of optimism. If a man could give birth at all, then surely anything was possible. We set our co-ordinates and turned up the stereo:

'At first I was afraid,
I was petrified . . .'

We would survive.

Georgina Starr

'TUBERAMA:
A MUSICAL ON
THE NORTHERN LINE
(OR HOW TO BE IN TOUCH
WITH YOUR EMOTIONS)'

I'd started the day off in a pretty good mood, but people were queuing up to give me a hard time. The guy in the record shop was disgusted at my request for Dougal and the Blue Cat's 'I Am The King of All The World', and told me to 'Fack Off' in a half-sarcastic yet offensive sort of way. His black corkscrew curls quivered around his head and I imagined that his irises were black behind his dark shades. Further down the same street a dead cat lay in the gutter. Squashed to pulp, its eyes had exploded like champagne corks and lay next to its corpse, looking like the balls on a swing tennis game. I wondered if I looked into the eyes I would be able to see its last movements still developing on the retina like a camera obscura. I swallowed hard.

A packed carriage on the tube. Sweaty armpits, farting bottoms, snotty noses and lecherous looks. Catching the eye of quite an attractive-looking bloke I move my head to see the magazine on his lap. After reading the cover — *Thrust Lust* — I fought hard to not look back at him. When he winked I felt a ripple of nausea in my chest. Seeing the naked bodies reflected in his glasses, I'm convinced that he's repressing some sort of sadistic impulse and I can almost picture the evil sex crimes he's already committed. He's probably based himself on that '70s horror movie where that guy murders women on the tube and takes them into his underground lair under Russell Square station, keeping them alive for years and crying and muttering 'Mind the Doors' (the only language he knows) when they finally snuff it. Before I get too carried away, I avert my eyes towards my bag and pretend to search for something. At King's Cross, Mr *Thrust Lust* gets off and I finally get a seat. A bead of sweat chases another down my back and I stare at the other passengers in disbelief. The lighting gives everyone a greenish tint, like a Boots photo with the exposure warning sticker on it. About five of them are either dead or asleep, slouched over with their faces stuck to windows and only their dribbles and nodding heads to prove they're actually alive. An old guy shuffles on, taking two steps forward and staggering almost one step back. Everyone stares and watches as he walks, like an old silent movie he's shaking like hell and it looks like the act of living is just too much for him. Thinking about it, I'm not actually sure if he's old or if he's one of those kids with that weird fast-ageing disease, with a mixture of Parkinson's and St Vitus' Dance thrown in. He sits down next to a guy who looks like he's walked right off the set of *Planet Of The Apes*. He's sat stroking his girlfriend's stomach while she stares upwards in a coma-like haze. Is she enjoying it? Is she blind and so unaware of her partner's resemblance to the Missing Link? Is she in love? There's a huge woman next to Ape Man's girlfriend. With flesh rolling over both arm-rests, she's reading a book on Physical Theatre while stuffing a Big Mac in her mouth, a new kind of theatrical movement. There's a smell which is a cross between animal fat and sweat lingering in the air, and I wonder if they're both coming from her direction. The train stops with a jolt and a crackly voice announces a delay: 'I'm sorry, but the train in front broke down and there's gonna be horrendous delays. What can I say? I mean, it's not my fault . . . I'm just really really sorry.' The driver tries desperately to crack a joke, but no one looks amused.

'TUBERAMA: A Musical on the Northern Line'

People start to chunter to themselves cursing and repeating the same words and some of the dead people wake up for a few seconds. The young woman next to me starts to scratch her hand manically as if she wants to draw blood. A guy in a suit applies a massive amount of Lipsil to his lips, and the man on my other side starts to roll a peach around in his hand as if it's a relaxation ball. What a bunch of no-hopers. As I focus in on these demonstrations of self-harm, I cringe at the idea of being stuck down here for days with this lot. I'd have to get to know them, we'd have to talk. Then I notice the guy from the record shop. This really worries me as he still looks in a foul mood. Sitting upright like a sub-human android, he's bound to turn psycho if we're trapped down here for a while. I can't work out if he's looking at me or not and I start to bite around the edges of my fingernails. With his Walkman headphones glued to the sides of his head, I'm convinced that he's definitely not 'one of us'. There's probably no music on the cassette he's listening to, it's just a series of instructions which guide him through his life here on Earth. He switches on every morning: get up, put on black leather pants, dark glasses and Rasta hair wig, light B&H and put in corner of mouth, play AC/DC backwards to piss off neighbours, get tube to work, abuse customers and generally freak people out. He's probably scraped that cat up from the street outside his shop and we'll be forced to eat it during a Satanic ritual he'll get us involved in. I try to stay calm and think rationally. If we're going to be down here for days someone will have to take control. Whoever it is will need to have words with whoever has the flatulence problem as air supplies will be limited. Maybe the fast-ageing kid, who's really shaking and jerking about now, will come into his own and rise to the situation. It's the chance he's been waiting for his whole life. He'll be our leader. He'll give us the confidence to go on.

In synchronization with the nervous blinking and nostril-twitching of a man opposite my mind ticks into action. The music begins, starting in a low key and building up to a higher one (like the tube as it picks up speed). From my seat I start to sing the introduction song:

Everything I See Makes Me Sad

As some offensive sights have vexed my eyes
So shall I start my song with such a question as —
Why does everything I do make me so sad?
And every turn I take turn out bad?
My mood depends on beauty in my heart
But as of late this beauty's taken its depart
Oh heavy is my heart and dark my thoughts
That winks and smiles and noises only serve to taunt
Why does everything I do turn out so bad?
And every turn I take makes me sad?
Everything I do makes life feel oh so tragic
It's time to weave a web of fiery magic
It's time to take the light and airy path
As living needn't be so dim and dark a picture
By chance the spinning web of drama
Could spin and turn a Tuberama (very high and reverberating)

As the music changes tempo and becomes much faster, there's a build-up of various instruments. Samples of noises from the tube are mixed in with the sound. Then suddenly the old kid throws off his beige duffel coat to reveal his gold and red Lycra outfit underneath. Like the priest in *The Poseidon Adventure* he jumps forward to take control, his voice is not a whimper but is strong and controlled: 'Rise up people – we must form groups and face our challenge. Be strong! We can survive this underground hell!'

His leadership speech turns into a lively song and dance routine which is the chorus to my song:

I've got the feeling we're moving!
I've got the feeling we'll be OK!

(Backing from other passengers still expressionless in their seats – *Odiodido fo diodido*)

It's like a dream that I'm feeling
It's like the feeling of being in love!

The Northern Line wooden floor is perfect for his tap routine)

You've been dreaming that you're living
It's time you were living out your dream!
It's time to love, to dance, to feel
Wake up! Don't fall asleep behind the wheel

Unbutton that shirt and loosen that tie
No need to walk when you can fly
You've been feeling life's such a drama
Yes it's time to spin and turn a Tuberama!
It's time to take the light and airy path
As living needn't be so dim and dark a picture

By chance the spinning web of drama
Could spin and turn a Tuberama.

With the song in full swing, there's another jolt and the tube miraculously starts to move again. It's going much faster than usual and speeds through tube stations without stopping. We catch glimpses of fantastic events inside the now-anonymous stations. A bar scene with bright red and green and an all-female dance troupe in white dresses. Silver balloons float around as they kick their legs and shake silver cocktail shakers in time to the music. Another station – a chorus line of ticket inspectors in bright pink uniforms are marching in synchronization down a long moving staircase, silver glitter falling all around them. We travel through strange dining rooms, dance halls, cafes, hospital wards and swimming pools. Each image blurs into the next like a flashback in memory of places we've been before. Back on the tube, Our Leader is now singing through a large silver megaphone. His voice echoes as if it's in a large empty space. As we career through the tunnels, the megaphone seems to grow in size. All the passengers are drawn into a spinning scene within the megaphone's mouth. I kneel on the seats and watch more changing scenes from the window. An underwater scene with grinning synchronized swimmers in blue water with pink bubbles, searchlight flashing through the water. A drive-in movie scene in the rain with only red cars and screaming couples, hands covering their faces as the light flickers from the horror scene on screen.

Scene after scene rushes by until suddenly I experience the ecstasy of a timeless moment. Everyone on the train is caught in the stillness of the instant. There's complete darkness outside, then after a few seconds a door at the top of a long staircase opens. A few notes on the piano introduces the song and an orchestra begins. The light in the doorway is emanating from a woman who has appeared at the top of the staircase. Her costume glows like one of those luminescent skeletons at a Christmas pantomime. As she starts to sing members of the orchestra float out of the door behind her, they're attached to threads which glisten in her light as they fly in the air and down the stairs playing their instruments. The lyrics of the song seem impossible to understand, it's as if they're in a different language yet it feels like something in the story she is telling is recognizable. It's like her words are untangling something as she sings. The light from her costume illuminates our carriage and awakens the girlfriend of Ape Man, who comes out of her coma like haze and starts to translate the song. It's as if there is some connection between her and the skeleton woman and her voice creates a backing narration to the song which is a slow number.

Am I More Lovely Than This Day?

Skeleton Woman: *Oobidobi swilliadow op ow obidobecow*
obido be dwilliyabop didibo oyacoo mop mop
fluctifluctdip sidiyatwee op ee
fluctifluct dip twee
fluctiflucdiptwee eetwee ah odo
oblahdi odwee ah ah . . .

Translation: *It's a story of the ability of humans to live on a lukewarm level from day to day, without intensity. It's about wishful thinking and unfulfilled fantasies. It's about the unreality of life. Holding onto threads. It's about not seeing beauty in the unbeautiful. It's about not delving into your soul. It's about not facing yourself and learning new ways and riding on different roads . . .*

Georgina Starr

Skeleton woman: *didleya boodan flopado bariba*
booyasuyavoodoo fooyaooyafooyaooya cuckoo cuckoo
cuckoo
obidoobi idiyabip op ip
obidobe flip
odidodee bidiadop
ovideo orideo mop mop

Translation:
He tried to compare me to a summer's day
But today the sun has gone and left Klee grey
Am I more lovely than this putrid day?
Am I more dark than clouds which warn of storms?
Am I more deep than pools of water underfoot?
Am I more cold than winds and fickler than these wind swept trees?
He said — Rough winds do shake the darling buds of May.
Does my face portray the harshness of this summer's day?
Am I as evil as the muddy puddles' spray?
Am I more cunning than the rainbow's gift of gold?
Do cows lie down in fields when I awake?
Do people run for cover when I call?
If not then don't compare me to this summer's day.
(She starts to cry)

Skeleton woman: *didleya boodan flopado bariba*
booyasuyavoodoo fooyaooyafooyaooya cuckoo cuckoo
cuckoo
obidoobi idiyabip op ip
fobidoobi flip
rudidodeebidiyadop
ovideo orideo mop mop

176

The song leaves everyone quite silent; as it ends the tube train is released from the tunnel and we're suddenly outdoors. It is a summer's day and the passengers run to the windows to catch the first pieces of daylight. The tube winds up through hills and small villages. We could be anywhere, Spain, Italy, Ireland, Germany or Austria, it's hard to tell. As we pass through a second, larger village we see a sign which reads WELCOME TO DOPPLESTAT. For a while there is no one around until finally we see a shepherd tending his sheep on a pasture. The shepherd looks quite familiar, although I'm not sure why.

For a few seconds, I'm convinced that I see what looks like me driving a car between the clouds beyond the hills. But when I look again, I'm gone. As we travel through the village we see more people who look vaguely familiar. At the very top of the hill we enter the gates of a large yellow castle with red flags on each of its towers and as we pass a sign for DOPPLE CASTLE we are pulled back underground.

The train travels slowly and the way is now lit by strange underground cells. Our Leader starts to whistle a tune which has a calming effect and various passengers join in to make a chorus of whistles. When the tube finally stops the doors open to the familiar sound of 'Mind The Gap' which is played at a higher speed than usual. We all clamber out, looking slightly disorientated. An odd-looking man appears out of the darkness. Looking like the Childcatcher from *Chitty Chitty Bang Bang*, he's wearing a tall black hat and stripy leggings and has a single painted red nail. We're led towards one of the dimly-lit cells, watching nervously as he unlocks the cage door. There's a group of people inside but they all have their backs to us. My heart starts to pound and I suddenly feel unexpectedly nervous and uncomfortable. Then to my surprise the man shouts, 'G-E-O-R-G-I-N-A!'

His voice echoes around the tunnel and I have a chalky taste in my mouth as the people slowly turn inside the cell. We all stare at their faces. The cell is full of people who look identical to me. Our Leader holds on to my arm to stop me from keeling over. Each of the replicas is wearing a T-shirt with various words on it. Their facial expressions seem to correspond to the words on their chests: Pain, Misery, Ecstatic, Lively, Scared, Irrational, Vulnerable, Doubtful, Discontentment, Hysteria, et cetera. Then the guy – who we find out is called The Emotion Catcher – suddenly starts to sing and the replicas answer his calls. When they are called they take specific positions and their replies have a voice delay sound which enhances the *doppelgänger* effect.

The Emotional Role Call

*A is for anxiety (*the replicas speak when they are called*): 'What?!'*
and ambition: 'I'm ready for anything.'
and G for guilt: 'What did I do? Just tell me what I did?'
and C for cruelty: 'I'm gonna twist your little head right off!'
T is for timidity: 'Shyness is nice.'
D is for disgust: 'Don't come anywhere near me!'
and doubt: 'I'm just not sure . . .'
H is for hysteria: 'What do you want . . . what do you want . . . what do you want?'
and hate: 'You're gonna suffer for this!'
X is for xenophobic: 'I don't recognize anybody . . .'
Y is for yearn: 'I need you, I need you, I need you!'
M for masochism: 'Please hurt me.'
misery: 'Unhappiness is a way of life.'

and melancholia: 'I'm a barrel of regret.'

E is for egocentricity: 'I am bigger than you'll ever be!'

I is for inhibition: 'I don't think I can go through with this . . .'

and irrationality: 'Here comes my body!'

and indecision: 'Have you ever had the feeling that you wanted to go,
then you had the feeling that you wanted to stay?'

J is for jealousy: 'My emotions are stronger than yours.'

K is for killer instinct: 'You wouldn't like me when I'm angry.'

and L for love: 'My heart is an over-ripe tomato.'

N is for neurotic: 'Who said that?'

and nervousness: 'What knife? Whose knife?'

Q for quiescent: '. . . murmur . . .'

and quixotic: 'Take everything I own!'

B is for brashness: 'Get a load of this!'

and boredom 'Knowledge is a curse.'

F is for fear: 'No! No!'

R for repressed: 'No way am I ever doing that!'

and resentment: 'I don't have to take this shit from you!'

P for paranoid: 'He's been following me all day. . .'

and pain: 'I'm dying inside . . .'

and pride: 'Such a lovely lovely word.'

and pity: 'You poor, poor thing . . .'

S for shame: 'I'm sorry.'

and for scared: 'MUMMY!'

and stupidity: 'Huh?'

suicidal: 'I'm defeated by life.'

seriousness: 'The mystery, like so many, was explained.'

and sociable: 'Live, live all you can, it's a mistake not to!'

and schizophrenic: 'What other half?'

U is for unique: 'The dead know only one thing — it's better to be alive!'

V for vulnerable: 'My knees are shaking.'

Georgina Starr

W for worry: 'To kill by strangulation?'
Z is for zoomorphic: 'Meeoooww!'
and O is for obsessive: 'O-Be-eS-eE-eS-eS-I-Ve-eE!'

As the song goes on he takes us around to the other cells which are filled with other *doppelgängers* of all the passengers in our tube carriage. On seeing their replicas, people are in shock but demand to know what is going on here in Doppelstat. The Emotion Catcher tries to calm us down and begins to explain, telling us first that he is a complex human being who craves simple answers to mysteries of the human mind.

'The Emotional Doppel Method,' he tells us, 'has been practised for hundreds of years. From the day you are born with every emotion you feel a new you begins to grow.' He tries to outline the procedure to make things clearer. 'Each emotion you express sends a signal to the Feeling Ray which is in our laboratories here in Doppel Castle.'

'But what does the Feeling Ray do?' Our Leader asks.

'The ray gives birth to a tiny replica which then grows every time you experience that feeling again. The stronger and more frequent the emotion, the quicker the replica grows. When it is fully developed it is taken to the Emotional Cells which we see here. The replicas which we have seen are the ones which represent your strongest emotions.'

He explains that each week one fully grown emotional replica is released into Doppelstat and is allowed to go anywhere in the world and live independently if it likes. I remember the replica that I thought I saw in the sky and ask him if it was me. He explains that the doppel I saw was my 'Oddness' emotion which was set free a few weeks ago, who drives through the sky in a red car singing to '70s pop songs. The other look-alikes we saw were also doppels which had been released. We all had hundreds of questions we wanted to ask, so he decided to take us to the labs so we could see the process in action.

The lab was a strangely melancholic place with hundreds of emotions bottled up inside glass jars of varying sizes. Like a mortuary and prison combined into one, rows and rows of little people were waiting patiently to become fully grown characters. Looking around at the other passengers it felt like some of the emotions would be here for ever. Taking a closer look at my own it was embarrassing to see which ones were only in their early stages of growth. 'Happiness' was waving frantically at me as I looked into her little glass home, and I knew it was time for me to change my ways. To make matters worse the Emotion Catcher started to tell us stories of where our fully developed emotions live and showed us slides of them in various places around the world. 'Well, Miss Starr,' he eventually said. ' "Depression" lives alone in Malmö in Sweden, she's a writer.' He showed a slide of 'Depression' standing outside a wooden cabin in the mountains, looking obviously quite low. ' "Indecision" lives six months of the year in LA and six months in the Outer Hebrides.' 'Indecision' was water-skiing in LA, speeding along in the water, then on the next picture she was buried in snow somewhere in the middle of nowhere. ' "Paranoia" runs a home security service in Switzerland, and "Neurotic" became a dancer in Brazil.' I ask if it's possible to meet some of our replicas and have a talk with them. 'But of course!' he exclaims. 'Why do you think we have brought you here? People, you are here to face yourself, to face your weakest emotion!'

Horror is emblazoned on all our faces as he goes on to explain that we will be able to take our weakest emotion home with us so we can help it grow. We're led through to another part of the lab where a large conveyor belt is turning. The Emotion Catcher presses a button which releases small jars which pass along the conveyor belt like small sushis in a Japanese sushi bar. We queue up and are each given a small jar like the presents at the end of a children's party.

Back on the tube the atmosphere has changed from earlier in the day. We all sit holding our emotion and smiling and chatting with each other. Unbelievably I was getting on well with Jeff, the guy from the record shop. He told me that he'd look out for the Dougal and The Blue Cat record and even went so far as to get a portable keyboard out of his bag and do a little rendition of the song to prove he knew it. It was good to hear it again. I was a bit surprised at his change of mood until I caught a glimpse of the label on his jar: 'Tolerance'. Everyone was really making an effort to talk to each other and I even heard people arranging to meet up. Ape Man had stopped rubbing his girlfriend's stomach because she was getting on really well with the guy with the Lipsil lips. They realized that their replicas were the same emotion and were talking about how they could make them grow. Ape Man looked pissed-off, but his replica was 'Coolness', so he was trying hard to control himself. The underground felt almost like a special place to be and I suddenly understood why the Madonna had visited it recently in Mexico.

Going up the escalator at Old Street, I took the jar out of my pocket for the first time. I had an idea what the little replica smiling and blowing kisses at me was without even looking at the label. Arriving home I looked up 'love' in the dictionary and sitting on my shoulder my replica began to sing in her lovely little voice:

182

'TUBERAMA: A Musical on the Northern Line'

All About Love

Get rid of the homely and the lonely
Wave goodbye to the hate, exfoliate!
It's time to start with amorous glances and seductive advances
To get out of control and get caught on a roll
Start looking for answers in smoochy dances
Hug cuddle and kiss, adore someone's lips
Watch your hands curl around waists and go back to their place
It's time to fall, can't you hear Cupid's call?
Go crazy! Start fooling around.

Go out tonight and fall head over heels,
Get blown away and ride high on a breeze,
Smooch, nibble and flirt, roll round in the dirt
Be the light of a life, not a trouble and strife
Don't be so closed and don't wriggle your nose.
Write love notes with pride, have a bit on the side
Find a ménage-à-trois and make love in a car,
Go get some sly looks in and then get your hooks in.
Go steady and spoon, play footsie and moon
Sail dreamboats and ride on cloud nine.
Be someone's love-fool, be love-struck not cool
Hear bells in the night and find love at first sight.
Feel your heart pound within, romance isn't a sin!
Go all the way, fall madly today.

Quote Romeo and Juliet, kiss, cuddle and pet
Speak of heavenly looks read romantic books
Let angels play strings of your heart.
Get hot and flushed cheeks, pine for someone for weeks

183

Georgina Starr

Ride on white horses and kiss between courses
Whisper in ears and love them to tears.
Notice that aura and just don't ignore her.
Watch the sunset in May and see The Green Ray

Look with stars in your eyes and with heavenly surprise
Let a blush bepaint your cheek and feel your knees go weak.
Let love's wings be your chair and its bosom your air
Get carried away, just go all the way.
I think it's your turn to get carpet burns
Let love be your water, adopt Cupid's daughter
Drown in its ocean and drink up its potion.

It's time to fall, can't you hear Cupid's call?
Go crazy! Start fooling around.

It all sounded like hard work to me and I knew I had a job on my hands. I'd have to nurture this little 'Love' replica like a mother would a child and make her grow so one day she'd be out there walking around, filled with love for humankind.

Guinevere Turner

'COOKIE AND ME'

It was a hot gross sticky July night in New York City and I was in no mood to go out. A whole group of us were going to dinner, mostly because our friend Ally was visiting from out of town. Everyone was acting kind of drippy and boring, except for Ally, who was chomping at the bit to settle down into some serious drinking. As dinner ended, each of my friends excused themselves because of tiredness or having to work or whatever, and I was left as the sole member of the entertainment committee. I took her to the most famous lesbian bar in New York, promising myself that I would leave after a drink or two. But Ally wasn't having it.

'Bartender!' she bellowed, slapping her hand down on the bar. 'This lady needs a drink — fast!'

She's the kind of person who will buy you a drink if you put yours down for two seconds and she was having a ball. Five Scotches later we were upstairs dancing our hearts out, and I think we even took our shirts off and danced in our bras, but I'm not sure because this is a story about a night I don't remember so well.

At four a.m., when I insisted to Ally that we leave before I slipped into a coma, we stumbled out on to the street. There was a cab already parked outside the bar, so I said goodnight to Ally and got in. The driver was a woman, which is a huge rarity in New York. She was a butchy Latina, really friendly and talkative. She immediately started asking me all sorts of questions — was that my girlfriend, did I go out with girls, why did I go out with girls, did some guy break my heart, etc? I was intrigued by this and started questioning her back — how long had she been a cab driver? Was she married? Had she ever had sex with a woman? In my confused state I decided that she was a married woman who deliberately parked outside women's bars late at night in an effort to secretly pick up a girl without her husband knowing. I became convinced of this. Unfortunately, I also became convinced that I would be the one to take her home.

I have spent years trying to convince my friends that this is absolutely unlike me — that this was the first and only time I'd ever tried to pick up a stranger. No one believes me to this day.

I tried my hardest to pick her up. I remember her insisting that she couldn't because she was working, and me insisting that it would only take half an hour or so. At the time that really seemed like a selling point. She had me going, though, because she kept driving me around and around and talking to me as if she was interested. I don't remember at all how it ended, except I couldn't believe she wouldn't take me up on the offer. Somehow I got up the stairs to my apartment and passed out. When I woke up the next morning I breathed a huge sigh of relief. Thank GOD she didn't come home with me — first, what a messy experience that would have been for her, and second, what the hell was I thinking? What would I have felt like if I woke up with the horrendous hangover I was dealing with AND the cab driver who drove me home was in my bed? I told my friends, 'You wouldn't believe what I tried to do last night . . .' and they all told me I should be careful, or I was going to get myself killed one day.

Seven months passed and the cab driver story became an old summer tale with hazy details. I was standing in a bar with a friend in January, when suddenly about five of my friends walked in looking like someone had died. 'I really have to talk to you,' one of them said in a sombre tone and I got freaked out.

'What? What's going on?'

'Remember that cab driver story you told us?'

'Yeah, yeah – why? Is she here? Is she mad at me? Is she someone else's girlfriend?'

'No, it's on TV.'

This didn't register for me at all. 'What do you mean, on TV?'

She took a deep breath. 'OK, there's this TV show, and they taped people in taxis last summer, a lot of people, and you're on the show. Everyone was just talking about it at this party we were at.'

Incredulous, I dropped to the floor of the bar in a foetal position.

My friend called down to me, 'It's on four more times.'

Ouch. Have you ever been really drunk and tried to get someone to come home with you? Have you ever just done something embarrassing when you were really drunk and felt pained about it in the morning, telling yourself that everyone else was really drunk so no one would remember? Now imagine it on video tape. Now imagine it on TV. Five times.

We all gathered to watch it the next time it aired. I was in fits. A narrator explained how it worked: '. . . We put five lipstick-sized cameras inside each taxi and the driver had an ear-piece from which we could communicate with him or her from a van that followed closely behind . . .' The first lucky person on the show was an insane transsexual who was screaming, 'Everybody wants my cunt! Every man in this town!' She was a mess. I was beginning to get incredibly nervous about what actual words I had used to pick up my driver, since it was evident that the show didn't have any problem with vulgarities. In between segments they showed legless men in wheelchairs on the night streets of Manhattan and prostitutes leaning into cars. They played REM's 'Everybody Hurts'. I don't know about everybody, but I was certainly hurting. I couldn't wait to see how I fitted into this delicious little representation of the underbelly of New York . . .

The minute I appeared on screen, slurring my address to the cab driver, all of my friends started screaming, then screaming at each other to shut up. The words 'Tuesday – 4:20 a.m.' were typed across the bottom of the screen, as if a crime was about to be shown. I ran out of the room, covering my ears from the sound of my own voice. I stayed in the other room, occasionally lifting my hands from my ears to hear my friends howling. Then they all started screaming, 'Come back! Come back! It's over!'

I shuffled back into the room, head hanging, barely able to speak out: 'How is it?'

One person said, 'It's not that bad. It's kind of cute, actually . . .' and another said, 'Oh my God. Oh my God.' Still another said, 'Were you on serious drugs that night, or what?'

They taped it for me and it wasn't until hours later that I was actually ready to watch it. It was pretty fucking mortifying, I have to say.

First of all, what a sucker I was. Obviously the cab was way too well-lit and when you watch Cookie DeJesus, for that was my dream date's name, you can see how premeditated the line of questioning was – and how easily I fell into the trap. I mean, I don't think they expected me to come on to her, but I don't think they were at all unhappy when I did: Second of all, Cookie didn't look quite like I remember her from that night. She was indeed an appealing woman in her way but later, when she went on talk shows, they would introduce her as 'Cookie DeJesus, mother of three and grandmother of five!' I wished I could draw a picture of what she looked like to me that night as I rolled around in the back of her cab. Not so much like a grandmother. 'So,' the talk show host said to her, 'you certainly had an interesting experience . . .' The audience chuckled softly. She said, 'I just wanted to pull the cab over and give her a big hug.' That's more embarrassing than if she wanted to pull the cab over and slap me. Hug? 'I think she really wanted me to be a sort of mother to her,' Cookie said, not unkindly. Mother?

Third of all, I didn't say a single vulgar word in the infamous cab ride, but what I did say was worse. Just creepy stuff that no one should ever know you said. It's not even how I talk; I was just trying to figure out what she needed to hear to come home with me. I can only thank God that when she said, 'So you just wanna go upstairs and cuddle?' I said, '. . . or whatever . . .' instead of saying 'Yes, my gentle sister.' One of the more horrible things I did was to describe my girlfriend at the time as '. . . big . . . and quiet . . .' and when Cookie asked if Ally was my girlfriend, I snorted 'No!' and then if Ally was just a friend, I barked out 'Hmph! Not even!' The *pièce de résistance*, however, is the last moment of the segment, when leaning wistfully against the window, I murmured, 'Just you and me and no one will ever know. No one will ever know.'

My dad wrote me a little card a few weeks later, saying '. . . Caught you on late-night TV the other night, just flipping channels. Talk about a coincidence! And talk about drunk!' I got calls from people I hadn't heard from in years, saying, 'Wow! Your career is really taking off!' and 'It's just so great to see a sexually aggressive woman on TV!' And of course there were the endless people who recognized me in the street. 'Hey!' the guy in the copy shop said to his co-worker. 'That's the girl from the taxi! Hey – did she go home with you?' Two of my friends have memorized the entire thing and will start whispering to each other, 'OK – you be Cookie – go!'

I don't know what I was supposed to learn from this experience, except maybe that anything can happen and nothing is sacred, things I already kind of knew. I will say this, though: if you're ever in a taxi in New York and you see that the driver's name is Cookie DeJesus, tell her to drop you off at my house. I'm sure she'll remember the address. I'll come downstairs with a wad of cash and say, 'Cookie, start driving. I've got a few questions I want to ask you.'

SUSAN CORRIGAN

Moved to London in 1990, holding a suitcase in one hand and a Walkman in the other. Immediately became a freelancer at *NME*, the world's best-known pop music weekly, later moving to *i-D* magazine, where she is now a contributing editor. A regular writer for the *Guardian*, she is also a pop-culture commentator and critic, curator and writer. *Typical Girls* is her first anthology.

BIDISHA BANDYOPADHYAY

Teenaged author, Oxford University undergraduate and ex-*NME* critic whose first novel, *Seahorses*, was published to widespread acclaim. A contributing editor to diaspora style magazine *Second Generation*, Bidisha writes extensively on gender and political issues; her essay on youth culture and the millennium was a highlight of Sarah Dunant's anthology *The Age Of Anxiety* (Virago). Bidisha is currently finishing her second novel.

JENNIFER BELLE

Jennifer Belle is the author of the novel *Going Down* (Virago, 1997) which was translated into nine languages and optioned for the screen by Madonna. She is an editor for the literary magazine *Mudfish* and is working on a second novel. She is twenty-nine years old and lives in New York City.

Contributors

POPPY Z. BRITE

Poppy Z. Brite has worked as an artist's model, a mouse caretaker, a stripper, and (since 1991) a full-time writer. She has published three novels and a short story collection. Her most recent project is the biography *Courtney Love: The Real Story*, to be published by Simon & Schuster (in the U.S.) and Orion (in the U.K.). She lives in New Orleans with her husband Christopher, a chef and food writer.

TRACEY EMIN

Born in Margate, Kent to a Turkish father and an English mother, Tracey's starkly autobiographical installations, sketches, writings and films are on display at her South London gallery, The Tracey Emin Museum. Her autobiography, *Explorations Of The Soul*, is a gripping memoir sold to art buyers in £100 shares. The Head Girl amongst young British artists, Tracey has risen to national and international prominence purely by being herself and is a passionate advocate of the artistic potential in all aspects of her life.

CHRISTA FAUST

Christa Faust is a Domina and fetish model. Her fiction has appeared in anthologies such as *Revelations*, *Splatterpunks 2*, and *Love in Vein*. Her hobbies include collecting vintage lingerie and tying pretty girls to railroad tracks. She lives in Los Angeles.

Contributors

KRISTIN HERSH

Singer and lyricist of 4AD Records' Throwing Muses who came to prominence in the late eighties as a teen mother singing about working-class domestic crises and her own mental illness. Now living in the middle of the desert with her two boys Ryder and Dylan, Kristin is working on the follow-up to her acclaimed solo album *Hips and Makers*. An extremely engaging and funny storyteller who has conquered many obstacles.

LAURA J. HIRD

Part of Scotland's literary renaissance, her contributions to lit-zine *Rebel Inc.* and anthology *Children Of Albion Rovers* prove that a young woman's point of view is no more fair or kind than a man's – just funnier. Has just completed her first volume of short stories for Edinburgh's Canongate Books, the publishing house responsible for launching the careers of Irvine Welsh and Alan Warner.

CHRISTINE KIESER

Born in St Paul, Minnesota to Catholic parents, Chris has contributed to Minneapolis grunge-zine *Your Flesh*, played bass in several local bands, and regularly extolled the virtues of Australian punk rock on her local public radio show. Currently working on her debut novel, she remains a catalyst of the vibrant Minneapolis music scene which produced Husker Du, Babes in Toyland and The Replacements. *Completely Overloaded* is her first published work of fiction.

Contributors

JOSIE KIMBER

Brighton-based writer and journalist whose contribution, *Having Myself A Time*, is her first published work. With camp sensibilities which invigorated Britain's early Riot Grrrl movement, hers is a theatrical talent which has lent itself to Super-8 film work, guerilla art installations at London's ICA and a novel planned for publication in 1998.

JENNY KNIGHT

Best known as the editor of contentious groupie fanzine *Slapper*, Jenny has been a bright spark on London's music scene since the beginning of the decade. A regular at The Shining Path spoken word events, her irreverent yet hard-hitting fiction has won admiration in dressing rooms and salons across the country. *Schering PC4 – A Love Story* is a sign of things to come . . .

AMY LAMÉ

Developed her larger-than-life drag queen's persona growing up with mall rats on the New Jersey coast; escaped to London's more hospitable environs in the early nineties. Began as a cabaret performer in the ICA's Live Arts stand and at Manchester's It's Queer Up North festival, teaching safe sex to gay men. Her club night, Duckie, led to modelling and presenting BBC 2's *Gaytime TV*. Amy also coordinates Britain's fabulously diverse Lesbian Beauty Contest.

Contributors

HELEN MEAD

Talked her way into music journalism at the age of fourteen to interview her then-idol, Adam Ant, for Radio One; kept the dialogue going as a contributor to *NME* where she was appointed section editor before the age of twenty. We became one nation under a groove thanks to her early coverage of Acid House, Primal Scream and the Madchester scene; after a stint at *i-D* magazine, Helen inaugurated the successful *Trance Europe Express* series of compilations. Now the director of the innovative Blood Records label, Helen shakes her tail-feathers worldwide but lives in London.

EMILY PERKINS

Author of the collection *Not Her Real Name* (Picador) and this year's winner of the prestigious George Faber Prize, Emily was a teenaged soap star in her native New Zealand; just think of her as the Anti-Kylie. Combining a distinctly literary bent with twenty-something verve and cool, Emily's debut novel is published later in 1997. She lives in London.

JENNY ROSS

The Sunday Show presenter's Pop Pilgrimages and rants have done wonders for the nation's collective hangover; her award-winning stand-up comedy is full of similar mischief and hilarity. Working continuously in radio and television since her discovery at 1996's Edinburgh Festival, Jenny will soon embark on another series of *The Sunday Show* and is currently developing a music programme for Channel Four.

Contributors

GEORGINA STARR

Fabulously inventive artist whose work is principally concerned with the interpretation of dreams, communication and memory; recent acclaimed shows at London's Tate Gallery, Minneapolis' Walker Art Center and a riotous comic, *Starvision*, have done much to enhance her tremendous international reputation. *Tuberama*, which appears here, will be adapted into the all-singing, all-dancing musical of her dreams some time in 1998. When not reconstructing her remembrances of pop culture, attempting telepathy with cats or pillaging thrift stores, Georgina writes incisively for many British titles including *Time Out* and the *Guardian*.

GUINEVERE TURNER

Actress, author, journalist and screenwriter whose 1994 lesbian comedy *Go Fish* was the highlight of that year's Sundance Film Festival. Recent film appearances include a lead role as a dominatrix in *Preaching To The Perverted*. In partnership with *I Shot Andy Warhol* director Mary Harron, Guin is currently writing two scripts: a biopic of fifties US porn icon Betty Page and the film adaptation of Brett Easton Ellis' *American Psycho*. She lives in New York.

Acknowledgements

1 'Talking in Bed' © 1997 Bidisha Bandyopadhyay
2 'Book of Nick' © 1997 Jennifer Belle
3 'Saved' © 1994 Poppy Z. Brite and Christa Faust; first printed in *Young Blood*, ed. Mike Bates, 1994.
4 'Albert Bert and Andy' © 1997 Tracey Emin
5 'The Snowballing of Alt.Rock' © 1997 Kristin Hersh
6 'The Boxroom' © 1997 Laura J. Hird
7 'Completely Overloaded' © 1997 Christine Kieser
8 'Having Myself a Time' © 1997 Josie Kimber
9 'Schering PC4 − A Love Story' © 1997 Jenny Knight
10 'Mapping' © 1997 Amy Lamé
11 'Wednesday Night, Thursday Morning' © 1997 Helen Mead
12 'The Indelible Hulk' © 1997 Emily Perkins
13 'The Immortals' © 1997 Jenny Ross
14 'TUBERAMA: A Musical on the Northern Line (or, How To Be In Touch With Your Emotions)' © 1997 Georgina Starr
15 'Cookie and Me' © 1997 Guinevere Turner